The Darkness Behind The Door

Copyright © Karen Oliver, 2012. All rights reserved. No part of this book may be reproduced or transmitted in any form or by any means, electronic or mechanical, including photocopying, recording, or by any information storage and retrieval system, without permission in writing from the publisher.

The Darkness Behind The Door

Publisher's Note: This is a work of fiction. Names, characters, places, and incidents either are the product of the author's imagination, or are used fictitiously, and any resemblance to actual persons, living or dead, events, or locales is entirely coincidental.

ISBN-13: 978-1-49368-215-7

Oliver, Karen, The Darkness Behind the Door

The Darkness Behind The Door

Karen Oliver

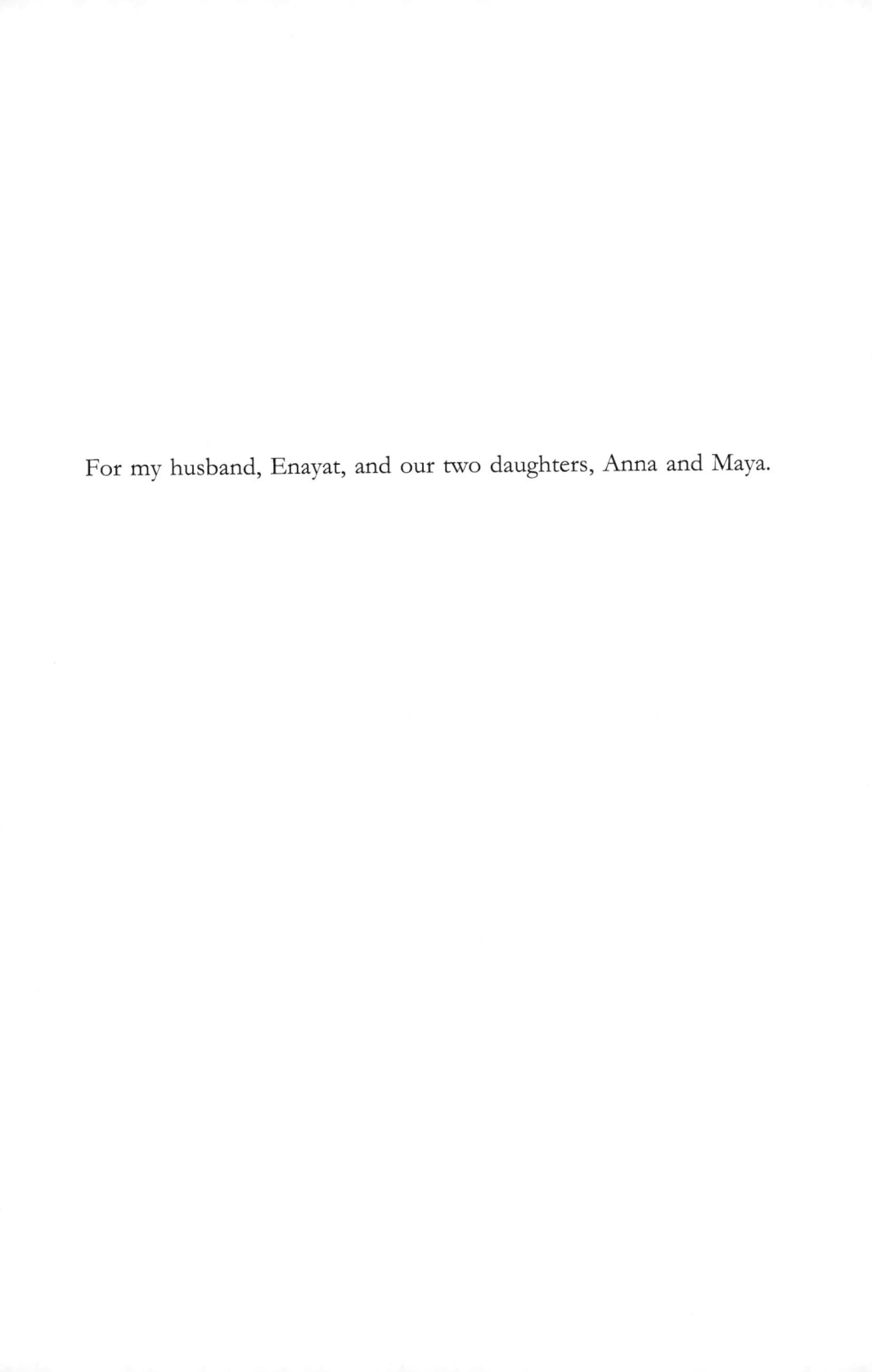

For my husband, Enayat, and our two daughters, Anna and Maya.

Table of Contents

Preface 9
Chapter 1 11
    Kansas City, Kansas, Christmas Eve, 2006 11
Chapter 2 35
    Hilton Head Island, South Carolina, 1975 35
Chapter 3 45
    Atlanta, Georgia, June, 2007 45
Chapter 4 49
    Hilton Head Island, October, 1975 49
Chapter 5 67
    Atlanta, Georgia, September, 2007 67
Chapter 6 73
    Corpus Christie, Texas, June, 1976 73
Chapter 7 83
    Atlanta, Georgia, October, 2007 83
Chapter 8 87
    Atlanta, Georgia, November, 2007 87
Chapter 9 95
    Hilton Head Island, South Carolina, July, 1978 95
Chapter 10 109

    Hilton Head Island, South Carolina, July, 1978 109
Chapter 11 117
    Hilton Head Island, South Carolina, August, 1978 117
Chapter 12 127
    Hilton Head Island, South Carolina, August, 1978 127
Chapter 13 137
    St. Thomas, U.S. Virgin Islands, March, 1979 137
Chapter 14 153
    St. Thomas, U.S. Virgin Islands, March, 1979 153
Chapter 15 161
    St. Thomas, U.S. Virgin Islands, March, 1979 161
Chapter 16 169
    Mobile, Alabama, November, 2007 169
Chapter 17 181
    Atlanta, Georgia, December, 2007 181
Chapter 18 195
    Atlanta, Georgia, December, 2007 195
Acknowledgements 205
Biography 207

Preface

Whenever I talk about my book, I always get the same quizzical look when I tell them it's about a serial killer. I know what they must be thinking. How did this middle-aged, suburban mother of two write such a dark story about a sociopath? In order to understand how this story came out of me, you would have to know about the dark time during which I wrote it. Most of it was written when I was pregnant with my second daughter and I learned that she has Down Syndrome. To say that the news was devastating does not really cover the fear and sense of loss my husband and I experienced upon hearing it. Finding out about her diagnosis felt like a death. I was never close to anyone who had a disability before, and the thought of my child having one was a completely foreign concept. I shed many tears wondering if she would ever grow up and live independently, if she would have the mental faculty to even know who I was, and yes, wondering if caring for her would destroy my marriage.

Not only was Maya's diagnosis terrifying, but the pregnancy was difficult as well. I broke my ankle during my sixth month. The pain of that along with the aches and pains of pregnancy added to my emotional distress. Knowing all of this then, it probably begins to make sense how such a dark character like Mitch Jordanger was created. Writing about him was my escape; it was how I pushed back all the emotions that were so overwhelming they made me feel like I was drowning. When I was writing, I was able to leave my broken body and live inside Mitch. Mitch didn't have a fragile baby growing inside him or a family in crisis because of it. He thought only of himself. What a relief it was to step into his world and forget my problems for a while.

    Now that Maya is here, I see everything differently. To say that she is a gift almost sounds trite so maybe it's better if I explain. She is a gift because of what she has given me, which is strength I didn't know I had. She has also taught me what a blessing it is to be completely able-bodied. I see her working to over-come her low muscle tone, (something people with Down Syndrome have that affects their ability to walk, talk, and even swallow) and I understand for the first time how lucky I've been to be able to do all of these things without thinking about it. Having her has awakened a spiritual feeling within me, too. I feel like God believed in me enough to let me take care of this special little person. I still worry about her future but somehow I know it will be O. K. That feeling is new for me, too, because I've always been a "glass half-empty" kind of person. With her, I have learned to take one day at a time and live in the moment. I celebrate her triumphs and know that tomorrow is another day to work on things she needs more practice with. I couldn't imagine a person with a purer soul than she has, and I wouldn't change anything about her even if I could.

Chapter 1
Kansas City, Kansas, Christmas Eve, 2006

She was one of those marginal people. The kind who crept into the open like a rat; driven by need and the cautious belief that no one was watching. She pulled up to the depressingly festive, dingy liquor store and parked her 1979 dark green Impala right in front. She bumped the curb, but the two bikers who sat nearby atop their bikes with cigarettes in hand didn't pay her any attention. She shuffled inside past a clerk who sat behind a counter that was trimmed with fake holly and a little silver Christmas tree. He barely looked up as her thick form moved to the vodka aisle and I knew then that she was the one. I knew she could disappear and no one would bother to look for her.

She paid for two large bottles of cheap vodka and headed back outside to the Impala. From where I was parked, I continued to watch her as she climbed inside her car. She opened one of the vodka bottles and took a long swig, then put the bottle down and began gathering her long, frizzy brown hair into a pony-tail at the back of her head. I got out of my rental car and walked over to the driver's side of the Impala and gently knocked on her window. I took care not to startle her, but she jumped at the sound anyway and spat some vodka out of her mouth. Annoyed, she glared at me through her window as she swore under her breath. I returned her glare with my best, most friendly smile. Still glaring and obviously unmoved by my charm, she wiped her mouth with her right hand and rolled her window down with her left.

"Merry Christmas," I said politely. "My name is Ma-"

"It's merry for some people," she interrupted. She looked me up and down irritably and then ignored me as she pulled her visor down to look at herself in the mirror. She sighed heavily as she took in her appearance and then roughly pushed the visor back into place. She grabbed the bottle of vodka again and took another long swig.

"What do you want?" she asked flatly.

"My name is Mark Goodman," I lied.

I held my hand out toward her window in an effort to shake hers, but she only looked at me with a sarcastic smile. I hastily dropped my arm and continued.

"I saw you pull up and wondered if you knew of a place besides this liquor store where I could get a drink? I was hoping to find somewhere to spend Christmas Eve besides my motel room."

She scratched the back of her head where the pony-tail was newly affixed.

"There's the *Alibi*," she replied, 'It's up the road about three miles from here, but it's probably not open."

"Where are you headed?" I asked boldly.

There was no point beating around the bush because I, literally, had a plane to catch. I had to get this woman to come with me in the next few minutes or else give up and head back to the motel. Melanie, my girlfriend of eighteen years, was waiting for me there. She worked as a flight attendant and she would be fired if she missed the plane.

Karen Oliver

Every Thanksgiving and Christmas for the past eighteen years, we flew to some sleepy little town together to spend our holiday. She did it to earn the extra pay, but my reasons were much more sinister. On every trip, I would slip away from Melanie to hunt, kill, and dispose of another inconsequential person. I had been successful this year when we spent Thanksgiving in Virginia, and I wanted to be equally successful in Kansas on Christmas Eve. On these trips, I always chose people who wore their disillusionment like a neon sign. They were so resigned to the disappointment of their lives that they had given up. I thought of them as a species of prey that was always searching for their predator. They seemed to be begging for a way out. Their loneliness called to me like blood calls to a shark. They were invisible to everyone else. Just like "Vodronika" was invisible to the bikers and the liquor store clerk. I had nicknamed the woman Vodronika the minute I saw her go for the vodka inside the liquor store. Now I tried not to show my disgust as I watched her downing the stuff like they weren't making it anymore.

"Why, I'm headed to a Christmas party at the Governor's Mansion," she sneered. "Where does it look like I'm going?"

In truth, she looked like she was going back to the hole from which she had crawled out. Her skin had a waxy, unwashed quality to it as though she hadn't bathed in weeks. She wore a dirty, over-sized fleece sweater that had a hood. Her disheveled ponytail hit it every time she turned her head. I noticed with dismay that she was heavier than I first realized. I had a bad back and it was going to be tough to dump her heavy body. All of these thoughts ran through my mind like bees crawling through a hive, but I forced myself to look relaxed and gave her another friendly, benign smile.

"Well, if you're free this evening, I'd like to buy you a drink at the *Alibi*," I told her. "And maybe some dinner, too, if they serve food there."

I tried to stay calm even though time was ticking by. I needed to get to the second phase of my routine if I wanted to make my plane and fly back to Atlanta with Melanie.

"I'm not looking forward to going back to my motel alone on Christmas Eve," I continued. "And you look like you're alone as well so I thought-"

Her eyes narrowed with suspicion

"I'm not going to your motel with you, Mister."

She practically spat the words at me, but she didn't crank her car to leave. I could tell she was weighing how safe she thought I was against how much vodka she thought I would buy for her.

"I'm sorry, that's not what I meant," I said in an effort to be agreeable. "I'm just looking for something to do on Christmas Eve, and I thought we could have a drink together. I got my Christmas bonus today, so I have plenty of money to spend."

She looked me up and down again and then blinked pointedly.

"Why are you alone on Christmas Eve anyway?" she asked suspiciously.

It was time to give my annual speech once again. I cleared my throat like a stage actor and hoped my performance would be believable again, like it was on Christmas Eve last year.

"I don't have any family, so I work on Christmas every year to let my co-workers be with their families. You see, my wife died a few years ago and the holidays have never been the same."

I hoped my speech would work its magic like it had so many times before and make me sound like a generous, sympathetic, all-around good guy. But speech or no speech, I had gotten this far with her so I knew from experience that she was coming with me. The promise of free liquor was obviously too good to pass up.

"Well, if you're buyin' then I guess I'll have a drink with you," she conceded. "That's if the *Alibi* is even open, but I meant what I said about your motel. I'm not goin' there with you, you got that?"

"Oh absolutely," I agreed. "But at least let me drive so you don't use up your gas." My heart pounded as I waited for her answer.

"Oh, I don't know about that," she replied skeptically but then her eyes narrowed greedily. "Give me some gas money and you follow me to the *Alibi*."

"How much?" I asked, disgusted but ready to play the game. We both knew what we were talking about now, and it wasn't gas money.

"Fifty," she said warily. She seemed to expect me to counter-offer. I didn't.

"O.K," I said without even blinking. "Let's get going."

"Give me the money first," she demanded.

"Twenty-five now and twenty-five after," I said.

She looked like the cat that swallowed the canary as I fished my wallet out of my pocket and handed her $25.00. She stuffed the money inside her bra and cranked the Impala.

"We'll take a left out of the parking lot up here and go about three miles," she said with the engine idling. Now that I had agreed to her price it seemed that she was the one who was in a hurry.

Fury was snaking its way across the back of my neck when the odometer on my rental car hit seven miles. I slammed the steering wheel as I watched the Impala weave from one side of the deserted, rural highway to the other without any sign of stopping. I didn't see any establishment called the *Alibi* coming up along the road, either. I was out on a limb already because of the time and if Vodronika didn't stop soon, I was going to have to turn around. I would have failed on Christmas Eve this year, and I'd have to wait another year before I could try again. The holidays were the only time I felt safe taking the risk because cities shut down and everyone, the police included, were preoccupied. I frequently *wanted* to kill, but I forced myself to wait until the holidays rolled around, and I was safely out of town. I was about to accept defeat and turn the car around, when at last the Impala's blinker came on and the car slowed down to make a turn. It wasn't the *Alibi's* parking lot that we pulled into; however, but a closed bar-be-que restaurant whose sign read *Slocum's*. As we pulled through, I noticed a set of wooden picnic tables and benches that sat inside a locked, screened-in eating area. A window with a sign over it that read ORDER HERE was closed and sealed off by an aluminum cover. I continued to follow Vodronika around to the back of the restaurant where she finally stopped the Impala. She killed her headlights and promptly got out of the car to walk back toward me. As I watched her thick form getting closer, I could already feel my back beginning to ache at the thought of carrying her heavy, lifeless body. Just then, a thin streak of lightening shot across the sky above her head and the wind blew her pony-tail back. When she opened my passenger door I could smell the rain in the air, but it was quickly replaced by the smell of cat urine when she slid into the seat next to me.

"Let's get this over with," she said blandly.

Her breath smelled like a mixture of cigarettes and the advanced stages of periodontal disease. She looked at me through bleary, blood-shot eyes and waited for me to tell her what I wanted. I couldn't imagine wanting anything from her except to put her out of her misery. Electricity ran along my scalp making my hair stand up and my eyes open wide. I lunged over the console and punched her hard right at her jaw line, slamming her into the passenger window. She reeled with pain and surprise. I quickly put my hands around her throat and began to squeeze. She was too shocked and injured from the blow to struggle at first, but as her oxygen began to slip away her instincts took over. She grabbed at my hands and desperately tried to push them away, but it was useless. She was no match for my strength. I squeezed and squeezed until I saw a peaceful calm come into her eyes. Transfixed by the look in her eyes, I didn't stop squeezing until several minutes after I realized she was dead.

   I didn't know how long I sat behind the bar-be-que restaurant with Vodronika slumped in the passenger seat beside me. Time seemed to have slipped sideways as though I had stepped into an alternate plane of existence. Everything receded and I felt calm and alone. I knew I had done the right thing by killing Vodronika. I had set her free. She wasn't going to have to scrape money together for vodka by selling herself to strangers anymore. She didn't have to worry about getting her teeth fixed, or having to take a bath. She was better off now and so was everyone else because she was gone. A crack of thunder snapped me out of it. I looked at my watch hastily. It was 6 p.m. Melanie would be frantic back at the motel. As a flight attendant she was required to check in early if she wasn't coming in from a connecting flight. I'd turned off my cell to make sure she couldn't reach me and I knew that when I turned it back on it would be full of tearful, angry messages.

   I pulled out of the restaurant parking lot with Vodronika slumped in the seat beside me and left the Impala where it was. I turned left and headed even further away from where Melanie, probably anxious and worried, waited back at the motel. The Kansas sky was turning dark and gloomy and the wind blew so hard that the cornstalks in the fields that lined the sides of the two-lane highway nearly flattened under its force.

Rain drops pelted my rental car, slicing sideways in the wind and coming down so hard that I could barely see. I had no idea where I was. All that was visible for miles was the deserted highway and corn fields in every direction. I raced to nowhere in search of a hidden place where I could dump her. I didn't dare leave her back at the restaurant because she might be found sooner than I wanted. If that happened, news of her death might trigger the memories of those bikers or the cashier at the liquor store. It would be much safer to dispose of her somewhere out of the way and buy myself some time before she was found.

I sped along the highway until finally I saw something promising. A tiny road peeked out from between planted rows of corn. I slammed on the breaks and idled on the highway trying to decide what to do. Surely this land was owned by someone, and this road could lead straight to their house. It was risky because trespassing was an easy way to get shot in rural Kansas. But on the other hand, it was the only secluded spot that I had seen in miles. I glanced at my watch; 6:45 p.m. We flew out at 10 p.m., so I didn't have time to keep searching. I made my decision and gunned the car to the right down the small, dirt road.

The rental bounced along through corn stalks and potholes; it was truly taking a beating. If the condition of the car were to be questioned, the storm would help explain the excess mud and there was a chance the heavy rain might wash some of it off. I probably wouldn't look too good myself and I'd have to change when I got back to the motel. I would tell Melanie I'd had car trouble and had to pull over to check a tire or something.

My blood began to boil again as I tore down the treacherous little road. Damn Vodronika for leading me so far away from the liquor store! Now I was lost and about to be stuck in the middle of a corn field. If I had to leave the rental car there it would serve as a roadmap for the police because I had rented it under my name. I glanced over at Vodronika and wished she was still alive so I could punch her in the face and kill her all over again. I angrily re-focused my attention on the road and pushed the car as fast as I dared. With every rock the tires hit or hole they splashed through the steering wheel jerked furiously. Vodronika's head bounced onto my arm and I savagely pushed it off, sending her flying into the window for the second time. At last I came to a small clearing where a tractor sat idly next to a small barn. It wasn't an ideal spot to leave her in because she wouldn't be hidden. She might soon be discovered by a farm worker or the landowner himself, but at least she would be miles away from the liquor store where I picked her up. Also, out in the open, the storm would help cover my tracks by washing my DNA off her body. I parked the car near the barn and resolutely got out into the rain. With raindrops pelting me, I hoisted her heavy body from the passenger side of the car and instantly felt my back seize up. I forced myself to carry her six feet or so and dropped her in a fit of blinding pain. She slumped to the ground and lay there with her eyes open amidst dripping leaves and little rivers of mud and water. My shoes had left footprints in the mud, but I always took the precaution of wearing a pair that were a full size too big and stuffed the excess room with socks. The footprints would not be attributable to me, and the shoes would go back with me to Atlanta where they would be disposed of.

Having dumped her in the narrow path between the corn stalks, I went back over to the car and opened the trunk. I took out a roll of paper towel, a pair of rubber gloves, and a water bottle that was filled with a mixture of water and bleach. The bleach would help break down any blood or fingerprints that Vodronika might have left. I got back inside the car and began to methodically wipe down the interior while rain hit heavily against the roof. With my back throbbing, I very carefully cleaned the window where Vodronika's head had hit and then went over the entire passenger door three times. Next, I wiped down the seat and console. I then tucked my paper towels, the water bottle, and finally my gloves into a plastic bag that was lying in the back seat. With the entire passenger side of the car clean and smelling of bleach, I decided to have one more look at Vodronika. After all, it would be another year before I would see that calm, non-seeing peace in someone else's eyes. I'd begun to dry off while I was inside the car so re-emergence into the cold rain was particularly unpleasant. I walked around to the back of the car and put the plastic bag that contained my cleaning supplies into the trunk. I slammed the trunk shut and then headed over to where she was lying. It was disappointing to see her again because she didn't look peaceful anymore. She was lying in an unnatural position and her eyes were open, looking upward, grotesquely oblivious to the onslaught of the elements. Looking at her made me feel disgusted again because she was so dirty. I gingerly reached into her bra and got my $25.00. I didn't want anyone to find it as it might lead them back to me. I stuffed it back inside my pocket. I took one last look at her and was glad I had cleaned the car so thoroughly. I didn't want even a trace of her to be left.

Back on the main road, I sped along and was lucky that no one passed me. I drove by the liquor store where I'd met Vodronika and barely gave it a look. Now that I'd reached my marker, it was time to call Melanie, and I dreaded it. I wasn't worried about convincing her of my story because God knew she was no intellectual. It never seemed to occur to her not to believe every word I ever said. No, it wasn't that I was worried about convincing her, but I wasn't in the mood. I was tired and my back ached and things had taken longer than usual. I wanted to get into some dry clothes and fly quietly out of town.

Melanie and I had been together for almost twenty years and though we weren't married, it was likely we'd be together for the rest of our lives. She'd been married and divorced and had raised a son, and though I'd never married I'd had my share of relationships. She was a good companion because we both like to travel, we were both essentially lonely, and she was naïve and helpless in a way that made my extracurricular activities possible. It wasn't that I didn't love Melanie; I did, it's just that I didn't respect her. But I was good to her, and I protected her from things that we both knew she needed protection from. She had been raised in the south in a time that didn't prepare her for managing her life when her husband left her. She'd been a semi-retired flight attendant when he walked out, and she'd gone back to it when she needed the money. Ever since her divorce, she volunteered for flights on Christmas and Thanksgiving for the overtime and holiday pay, and I had accompanied her on every trip for the past eighteen years. We had never been lucky enough to go anywhere that was fun during the holidays, like New York or Chicago. Instead, we always ended up in a sleepy, rural town. Everyone in these places had already settled in to spend time with their families, leaving me and Melanie to make the best of it in some rundown motel. I was never into the holidays much, so I didn't care where I spent them, but after the first trip I dreaded them because it was so boring. However, once I started using them to hunt and kill some used up person who didn't want to make it to the New Year, I couldn't wait for the next one. Melanie never caught on to what I was doing because she was easy to distract, unlike my friend Lauren. Lauren and I had met at work. I'd only known her for eight months, but I still understood that she was too savvy to believe the things I told Melanie. I knew that if Lauren was the one who was waiting for me back at the motel her sharp, nearly telepathic mind would read right away that I was full of shit.

Lately, I found myself wanting a deeper connection with Lauren. I wanted to tell her what I did on my trips and about other things in my past. It could be unsettling to be around her because she seemed to sense the truth. Her quiet eyes always looked at me like she knew what I was thinking. The time on my cell phone read 8:15p.m. Melanie should have checked in at the airport already. Without bothering to listen to her inevitably hysterical messages, I hit the button for her number in my cell phone and listened to it dial.

"Where are you?!" she screamed as soon as she picked up.

"Calm down, babe. I had some car trouble in the rain. I was working on it and didn't hear the phone."

"I thought you'd been in a wreck!!!!" she wailed.

I kept my voice calm despite my very strong urge to hang up.

"Well, I wasn't. I'm on my way and I'm almost there. Get some dry clothes out for me and we'll leave as soon as I change. It will all be O.K., hon-."

"I thought you were in a wreck!" she screamed again. She was nearly incoherent, but through her sobs I heard words that made my blood run cold.

"I, I c-called the police!!!!" she stammered.

I could tell that she was well on her way to that place in her head that she went to when she was overwhelmed. I had more patience for it at times than I did at others, but just then I really needed to know if the police were looking for me. I couldn't afford to lose it and have her not speak to me for hours as punishment.

"Melanie, tell me exactly what you've done. Tell me what you told the police."

She continued to sob and said nothing. I was afraid that she would drop the phone and I wouldn't get any information. I might be pulled over any minute or drive into an ambush of blue lights and sirens when I reached the motel.

"Melanie, I'm sorry I upset you, babe. It couldn't be helped." My calm voice belied my growing fury. "I'm soaking wet because I had to look under the hood in the rain, but everything is fine now. Don't cry; I'm on my way to the motel now."

"W-we're going to miss the plane," she cried.

"No, we're not. The airport is barely five miles from the motel, and there is absolutely no traffic on the roads. Heck, the flight is probably delayed anyway so we'll have plenty of time." An uneasy feeling came over me as I realized that the flight might be cancelled because of the storm. "It's all going to be fine," I continued, trying to sound light-hearted. "Now, babe, what did the police say?"

"They told me there weren't any wrecks that matched that rental car's make and model. They said they wouldn't do anything until you were gone for forty-eight hours."

Her voice had calmed, but I could still hear her soft sobbing. I breathed a sigh of relief to hear that the police had pushed her off.

"Well, I'll be pulling into the parking lot any minute now. Pull out some dry clothes for me so I can change and we'll head straight to the airport."

"You promise you're almost here?" she sniffled.

"Yes, I'm right down the street. Get my clothes ready, O.K.?"

"O.K." She sniffed again and hung up.

The rain was slowing to a drizzle when I pulled up in front of our motel room. A heavy curtain swung to one side and Melanie peered at me through the room's large, picture window. She opened the door as I made the short walk from the car to the room and leaned against it petulantly to let me enter. Her eyes were red from crying and her navy blue uniform was crumpled. Behind her, our suitcases were packed and ready to go except for one pair of jeans and a shirt that had been placed on the un-made bed. A dry, white towel lay on the bed beside the clothes but she had neglected to pull out socks and underwear.

"Sorry I made you worry," I said as I unbuttoned my wet shirt and pulled it off.

"Just hurry up; we'll miss the plane."

"Did you call the airline? Is the plane late?" I asked while I towel dried my hair. My real concern was that the flight was cancelled. It was high time I got the hell out of Kansas.

"I didn't call," she replied twisting her hair. "I hoped you'd be here any minute."

Dressed in dry clothes and with Melanie in the passenger seat this time, I drove the short distance from our motel to the small Kansas City airport where red lights lined runways and planes intermittently took off or came in to land. Melanie didn't say anything about the strong bleach smell during the short trip we made. She was probably too worried about missing the plane to notice. Being late just once was a fire-able offense in her line of work, and I could only guess what they'd do to her if she actually missed a flight. It was a miracle to me that Melanie, who was usually so scattered, could consistently make it to her job on time.

At last, we pulled into the parking lot of the car rental building. It was a small, cement structure with large windows that were decorated with red and green Christmas lights. A large white sign in one window said **MERRY CHRISTMAS 2006** in red and green letters. I parked the rental under a thin slab of a carport styled roof that was supported by metal poles. Large Christmas wreaths with big red bows were affixed at the top of each pole. Their felted ribbons flapped in the stirring breeze. I didn't see anyone working behind the counter. I was about to leave the key in the ignition and head over to check-in when a kid of about twenty came out through a door that had a sign on it that read "Employees Only". He waved, and I began to pull our suitcases from the trunk as he approached.

"Good evening, sir! You folks flying on Christmas Eve?"

I'd never heard that one before in the last eighteen years.

"You guessed it," I replied dryly. "We're in a hurry; any way to speed this up?"

"You bet, sir. Just leave her here and you can head over to check in. Which flight you on?"

"Melanie, which flight?" I asked.

Melanie looked at me with her typically vacant expression.

"What is the flight number, Melanie?" I repeated. God help anyone unfortunate enough to crash on a flight with Melanie as their flight attendant. Their odds of survival would be severely diminished.

"5173," she said at last.

"You know anything about 5173?" I asked, looking back at the kid.

"She's late. You have about forty-five minutes."

I relaxed a bit. "Well, in that case we might as well do this by the book. I didn't fill up the tank. Just charge my card for that."

"Certainly, sir. It's too bad, though, since we charge so much for the gas. I'll look her over real quick so you can sign off on the agreement and be on your way."

He moved to look inside the open trunk and my heart skipped a beat. I'd forgotten to dispose of my plastic bag with the cleaning materials inside! Before he could touch it I quickly reached over and grabbed it.

"Uh, sorry," I said to his startled face. "It's just some garbage I forgot about. I'll get rid of it."

He nodded bemusedly and checked something off on a list that was attached to his clip-board. He walked around to the passenger side of the car and took a seat inside. I watched as he opened the glove compartment and ash tray, and then checked the rear-view mirror. I held my breath when I saw him lean down to reach for something in the back-seat floorboard.

"Ma'am, you're forgettin' your charm. Maybe it fell off your bracelet?" He held up a small, knotted heart charm and I felt my blood turn into ice.

"That's not mine," Melanie said. She looked at me curiously but not accusingly. She always seemed to be in a dream.

"Maybe it's from the people who rented the car before us?" I offered.

The kid looked perplexed. "Could be, I suppose. Doesn't make sense, though." He shook his head lightly.

I wanted him to elaborate on why it didn't seem possible that the knotted heart charm could have been left by someone other than us. I wanted to grab it from him, punch him in the face, and run for the plane. I knew who the charm must belong to, but for the life of me I couldn't remember if she'd been wearing it. What else might be inside that car that I had missed?

"Anyway, are we good here?" I asked.

"Well, she's awful muddy, you understand, so we may have to charge you a cleaning fee."

"Is that really necessary? It couldn't be helped in the storm." I didn't really care about the cleaning fee, but I thought I should protest in order to avoid arousing suspicion.

"I understand, sir. These companies charge for everything they can. But you see, we just gave her a deep cleaning and this is her first time back out. Looks like some mud got into the trunk so we may have to shampoo her. Also, there's corn in the axles. Looks like you been ridin' in a corn field!" He smiled, but I didn't smile back.

"How much is the cleaning fee?" I asked with mock annoyance.

"$100.00 at most. Could be less, but you see, you got all this corn in the axle and.....".

"Well, whatever," I said cutting him off. "We've got to get to our flight. Just give me the agreement." I scribbled my name, *Mitch Jordanger*, and handed the clip-board back to him. Melanie seemed to wake up just at the wrong moment.

"What about your car trouble? They shouldn't charge us a cleaning fee because you had car trouble."

The young man's eyebrows rose.

"Well, I thought I had some trouble with the tire but it was O.K. Look, we've got to get to our plane. Charge me for the cleaning fee or whatever you need to do, but we've got to go."

He stood there mutely. I was sure he figured the tire problem was a result of whatever put all the corn in the axles and I didn't want him doing a more thorough inspection. I grabbed Melanie's arm a bit too roughly and began walking toward the airport entrance where I saw a sign that read "Baggage Check-In".

"Damned Ford's," I said to convince Melanie we'd gotten the short end of the stick.

Melanie walked quickly at my side and looked down at her feet. "No wonder...," she said.

"No wonder what?" I retorted.

"No wonder the police didn't find you. I told them you were driving a Chevrolet."

Back in Atlanta, in the comfortable home I shared with Melanie and her ten cats that I was deathly allergic to, I found myself unable to sleep. That wasn't unusual. Melanie, on the other hand had no trouble. She lay in our bed beside me snoring her familiar, light snore. I looked at her in the moonlight that was coming in through the skylight of our 1970s contemporary style home and resented her for sleeping so soundly. My back was killing me from carrying Vodronika's heavy body just like I knew it would. I should have gotten my prescription for muscle relaxers filled before I left for my trip, but I didn't have time. I sighed as I looked around the room because I knew it was going to be a long night. Instead of waking Melanie, I decided to hobble downstairs to my office where there was a bottle of scotch and hopefully some Xanax as well. They would numb my physical pain, and hopefully they would numb my mind and help me get to sleep. I grimaced as I got out of bed and hobbled out of our bedroom. On the stairway, I held the railing tightly as I eased myself down the steps. When I got downstairs, I didn't turn on the light in my office because of all of the moonlight that was streaming in through the windows. Instead, I leaned against my desk and shakily fumbled around in the drawer until I found the Xanax. I ate two pills with a long swig of the scotch and carefully eased myself into my executive chair. I sat hunched over in pain and quickly took one shaky drink after another. I felt very old when I caught the sight of my reflection in the window. I looked every bit of the fifty-three year old man I had become. Now that I was getting older, I was becoming acutely aware that something was missing. I thought about it during many sleepless nights while Melanie slept upstairs. I wanted to feel a real connection with someone. Melanie's gullibility made things easy for me, but sometimes I wished she knew the real me. I wanted her to know I'd spent our holidays hunting and killing instead of carving a turkey or shopping for gifts. I wanted to tell her the truth for once, and have her accept me for who I really was. I resented her because I knew she wouldn't be able to handle it, and I fantasized that maybe Lauren could. I wanted to tell at least one of them about all of the dark things I'd done, starting with the first murder I committed when I was just fifteen years old.

Whenever I let myself think about it, the memory was so vivid that I could smell the chlorine in the pool at the community center where it happened. I had been thrilled that summer when I got the job as a lifeguard. There weren't many jobs to go around in the rural town I grew up in, so landing it made me the envy of my friends. Another bonus was that my girlfriend, Shelly, swam at the pool so I got see her almost every day. But my real reason for getting the job was that I was saving for a guitar. I was so proud to be earning my own money that I didn't even mind that I had to clean the pool at 6 a.m. every morning. Or that I had to straighten up the locker room every evening before we closed. After a while my buddy Matt complained that he was bored. We had both figured out that we were glorified babysitters for parents weary from their kid's summer vacations. But I didn't care. I was still thrilled to have the job.

For weeks I enjoyed working at my job and counting my money, but that changed after the heavy-set man with thick, black glasses and a squared-off crew-cut started coming to the pool. I didn't find him very interesting at first, but it was my job to keep an eye on everyone, so I began to notice him. After a while his behavior struck me as odd. He never brought any kids of his own to the pool, but he always stayed in the shallow end with the little kids. He wore an inner-tube around his waist even though the water was so shallow that he could stand. I wondered why an adult wanted to hang around other peoples' kids. All the adults I knew wanted their kids to leave them alone. Something was off, but I didn't know what it was. As my suspicion grew, I watched him more closely until one day it hit me like a steel blade. It wasn't so much that I *saw what he was doing*, it was that I suddenly *understood*. He was using his float to hide that he was touching the kids around him under the water. Once I realized what he was doing, I saw how scared and powerless the kids around him were.

I felt powerless, too. Times were different then. We didn't talk about pedophilia or molestation openly and the shame I felt for doing nothing about it grew. Even worse, I was forced to watch because I was the lifeguard. Children swam around him all day like baby seals swimming around a shark. I began to dread going to the job I had liked so much. It had represented independence in my young life, but now I wished that the summer was over. On the days when the man didn't come to the pool, I was so relieved that it made me angry. My anger grew and grew until my blood boiled every time I saw or thought about him. I began to fantasize that he would die.

One day I got lucky. The community center was closing in an hour, so it was time to check the locker room for discarded towels. I was finishing up when I heard someone come into the locker room. It was the **man;** the disgusting, ruddy-skinned, fat bastard who had haunted me for weeks. He was completely nude as he had apparently just come from the showers. He did nothing to cover his nakedness as he walked through the dank smelling locker room. He saw me and to my horror, he became erect. I turned away from him and pretended to check a locker, but he came up behind me. He stood so close that I could feel his hot breath on the back of my neck. I wanted to run, but I couldn't move. Blood pounded in my head and hatred ran through my veins. I felt his hand on me but just then a toilet flushed, signally the man that we weren't alone. He stopped whatever it was that he was about to do to me and ran his hand along my shoulder. He made a show of turning around and walking back into the shower area. It seemed that he wanted me to follow him.

He disappeared around the corner, but I stood frozen where I was. I hadn't done anything, but I felt ashamed. I wanted to kill him. At fifteen, I knew I wasn't much of a threat to a grown man, but I was filled with enough hate and revulsion to lift a semi-truck. As I stood there trying to decide what to do a strange sensation came over me. The room seemed to tilt sideways and I felt like I was going to pass out. I closed my eyes and put my hand on the row of lockers in front of me to steady myself when I heard a loud *thud*, and a cry of pain. My eyes shot open and I looked around. At first I couldn't believe I had really heard anything but there it was again, the cry of pain this time followed by a muffled plea for help. The man must have slipped on the wet, cement floor in the shower. My heart pounding, I walked determinedly into the area where he had gone, but I didn't see him. I followed the moans of pain until I found him inside a shower stall where he had apparently been waiting for me. He was lying on his stomach and blood was spreading from underneath his face. I grimaced as though I was about to pick up a dead rat and rolled him over onto his back. His nose was crushed and his teeth were broken. A large knot was forming between his eyes. He was barely recognizable. With every breath he struggled to take he made a sick gurgling sound. I had been trained in first-aid so I could get the job as a lifeguard, and I figured that the gurgling sound he made was because his broken teeth were blocking his air-way. I knew what I needed to do to help him and possibly save his life. His teeth needed to be removed from his air-way and he needed to sit up so his head would be above his heart to slow the bleeding. But as I stood over his nude, gurgling body I knew I wasn't going to help him.

"Die, you **sick** bastard!" I hissed. **"That's** what you get for what you tried to do to me! That's what you get for what you've been doing to those kids in the pool!"

A black bruise was forming underneath each one of his eyes, but in those eyes I saw his surprise. He recognized that I knew he'd been molesting the kids in the pool by using his inner-tube for camouflage. In desperation, he pawed helplessly at my feet and tried to ask for help between gurgles. Disgust washed over me. Before I knew what I was doing, I lifted my leg and kicked him in the throat with everything I had.

"That's what you ***get!***" I hissed again.

He shuddered with pain and put his hands to his throat. His gurgling grew louder and his breathing became more laborious. As I stood over him, I felt like my brain was splitting into shards of glass like a windshield that had been shot out by a rifle. I nearly panicked when I realized that he might not die. He would tell everyone what I had done. I squeezed my eyes shut and prayed that he would die. Then, all at once, he stopped breathing. I opened my eyes and looked at him closely. I had never seen a dead person before. His desperate, pleading eyes had become strangely calm. In the place of his horrific gurgling there was peaceful quiet. I was free of him and so were the little kids in the shallow end of the pool. I learned something then. I learned that I could make things better by killing people. Instead of feeling guilty, I felt justified. Fate had shown me that there were people in the world who deserved to die, and I had the wisdom to decide who those people were.

I felt like I had been freed from the rules other people live by, but I was still haunted by what the man tried to do to me. I withdrew from my family and friends because I knew they wouldn't understand. They continued to go around like their problems were the center of the universe, but I had *killed* someone. I didn't feel like I lived in their world anymore and there was no going back to it. All through my teenage years, I fantasized about killing again. I became convinced that I was supposed to eliminate people who were too evil, too arrogant, too stupid, or just too annoying to be in it. I decided that population control would be my gift to the planet. I was filled with a sense of purpose, but I still understood that it was wrong. Killing the man had liberated me, but it had also sparked a dark urge that grew and festered inside me.

I took another long swig of scotch and let my hand run along a stack of rare vinyl records that I was organizing to take to my record store to sell. I thought of Vodronika back in Kansas. She was probably still lying in the rain and being munched on by rodents. I was glad that she was dead and happy to be hundreds of miles away from her in my warm home. Suddenly, I sat straight up in my chair despite the pain. Vodronika and I were really a lot alike! I had looked down on her because she was flawed and lonely. But I was lonely, too, and probably more flawed. Had Vodronika been successful and in love, once, like I was when I was young? Had she somehow gotten lost, and was I getting lost, too?

Fortunately, the scotch and Xanax were starting to do their job. My back had eased off and I was getting sleepy. I relaxed into my office chair and let my head roll around on my chest. I stared out of the window at the dark trees standing in the cold night and remembered a warm breeze on a gently rocking ocean. My mind took flight. When I was a young man in my twenties, there was a brief period when I could have changed the path I started on at fifteen. At that time of my life, I was a popular musician whose band was on the brink of success. I lived in exotic places and enjoyed a life that was filled with women, friends, and good times. I closed my eyes and let the faces of those I had known back then dance before me. I began to dream of myself as the person I used to be.

Chapter 2
Hilton Head Island, South Carolina, 1975

It was a hot summer evening, and I was twenty-two years old. My houseboat, the *Polargo*, was tied up at a dock in Sea Pines Cove, a sheltered bay off the Atlantic Ocean. I was drinking beer and watching the sunset when Eric and Lela arrived. I welcomed them aboard even though they weren't expected until the next day. I wasn't prepared for how beautiful Lela was, and it made it even easier to dislike Eric. They were both tanned and slightly drunk and maybe a little high. They giggled and whispered together as though they shared a wonderful secret.

I brought out some wine and walked over to where the two of them sat on deck-chairs. We sat together and drank the wine while the *Polargo* rocked gently in the rising tide. Mia had come with them, but she didn't join us. After we were introduced, she had politely excused herself and went over to the starboard deck on the opposite side of the houseboat. I knew I was expected to talk to Mia, but I was stunned by Lela so my efforts to draw Mia in were going to be half-hearted.

Lela stretched her long legs out and placed her feet on the *Polargo's* railing. She wore white shorts and a red and white striped top. Her gold earrings dangled along her neck. Sometimes they were visible through her blonde hair when she turned her head to laugh at one of Eric's stupid jokes. When we finished the bottle of wine, I went into the kitchen to get another one. Through the window I spotted Mia out on the starboard deck alone. She looked scared out there by herself, so I walked outside to talk to her.

"Mia, can I get you a glass of wine?" I asked as I held up the bottle for her to see.

"No thanks," she said as she clung to the railing and warily looked down at the water. "I'm good."

Maybe she was shy, but it seemed like she wanted to be by herself, so I was off the hook. I took the wine and headed back over to where Lela was. She was laughing naughtily as Eric whispered something in her ear. He flashed me a satisfied grin as I approached.

"We didn't ruin any plans for tonight did we, Marty?" Eric asked conspiratorially. He was trying to be smooth in front of Lela.

"Not at all," I replied. "What's the difference between tonight and tomorrow morning?"

I sat down and proceeded to open the wine. I filled Lela's glass and my own, and then handed the bottle to Eric to fill his own glass. She looked at me all the while. I kept my eyes trained directly on hers in return. I could tell that she knew what I was thinking. Eric, stoned and a bit slow on the up-take, didn't realize how Lela and I were looking at each other. He rambled on, but we stared at each other almost without blinking. She smiled a slow, knowing smile and took a sip of the wine.

"It's good," she said softly and goose bumps ran up the back of my neck.

Eric interrupted by putting his arm around her. He accidentally hit the wineglass she was holding and caused some wine to slosh over the side. She was annoyed by his clumsy move, but she only looked down and then back up at me and smiled her cat like smile. Suddenly, a scream shattered the peaceful evening calm. It sounded like it came from where Mia was on the other side of the houseboat. I jumped up, knocking over my wineglass. Lela and Eric sat up in their chairs; startled. I ran through the open sliding glass doors on the portside and then through the open set on the starboard side. I'd left both sets open to allow the breeze to circulate through the houseboat. At first I didn't see Mia, but as my eyes adjusted I saw that she was cowering against the wall of the boat. She had scooted as far away from the railing as she could get.

"Mia, what is it?"

"I saw something **there**; in the water!" She pointed at some reeds that floated carelessly in the current.

"What did you see; a fin? It was probably just a dolphin. Whatever it was, it can't hurt you."

"No, that wasn't it!" she cried and ran over to cling to me.

Eric and Lela came up behind me. I couldn't see Lela's face but I wondered if she was displeased to see Mia in my arms.

"It was *pink*!" Mia wailed.

"Mia, what did it look like?" Lela asked.

"I don't know. It came up and floated a long and then dove or sank! It seemed to be *looking* at me!"

"Look, Mia," I began, "nothing in that water can hurt you. Nothing that's pink anyway. Come and have a glass of wine with us. There's no reason for you to be over here by yourself."

I awoke early the next morning to make breakfast for everyone. Mia had stayed in a room by herself, and Eric and Lela had shared one of the larger bedrooms. After Mia's outburst my connection with Lela was severed. We didn't look at each other much anymore, and I did what I could to make Mia feel comfortable. When Lela went to the bedroom with Eric, I barely looked up. I'd felt something close to hatred for her.

However, I was pleased when I saw that Lela had gotten up early, too. She was standing at the rear deck next to the ladder that led up to the roof. Her yellow sun-dress blew gently around her tanned legs in the morning breeze, and her blonde hair was pinned back in a pony-tail. I pulled the frying pan off the stove and went outside to talk to her. She turned when she heard me walk up behind her and gave me a smile when I got close. I wasted no time finding out what I wanted to know.

"Are you and Eric serious?" I asked.

She smiled that slow spreading smile that already had come to drive me crazy. "A girl like me is never serious about anyone," she replied.

"That could change," I said.

"Could it?" she asked. "You think you could change it?"

I leaned in and kissed her. She didn't resist. I didn't step back from her until I got the feeling that someone was watching us. I looked over my shoulder and saw Eric looking back at me through the kitchen window. But, I didn't give a damn. He was going to find out soon enough that Lela was staying with me and he was leaving. After breakfast, a decidedly tense meal that was punctuated by Eric's forced attempts at being jovial, he announced that he and Lela were going on an excursion. He responded mysteriously when I asked where they were going.

"Trying to come with? Hang out here and show Mia some of that hospitality you were showing Lela this morning."

"Can't take the competition?" I asked sarcastically.

"Lela's free to do what she wants and it doesn't matter that much to me, you understand. But, I'm here to have a good time and I won't be trading Lela for Mia until I'm ready."

"Lovely way to look at it," I replied, disgusted. Eric was truly a pig. I couldn't say I'd never used a woman, but Eric had no depth beyond that. Lela didn't seem like the type who needed rescuing, but she could do better.

A few hours later they untied the two kayaks I kept floating behind the houseboat and paddled out into the bay. I didn't argue with Eric about it anymore and I didn't try to talk to Lela about it, either. I had gotten tired of all the tension, so I decided to take Mia to downtown Savannah. It was just under an hour's drive from where I was moored on Hilton Head Island. We could eat seafood and drink beer to ease the heat of the day and there was plenty to do and see. She could shop if she wanted, or we could take a carriage ride through the squares of the downtown area. I figured that it would be more fun for her than staying on the houseboat, because being on the water seemed to scare her.

We smoked some weed in the car during the drive to Savannah. Mia was pretty quiet both before she got stoned and afterward. This was fine with me. I quite appreciated a woman who didn't talk a lot. Being with Mia wasn't exciting like it was with Lela, but she was turning out to be good company. There was something sad about her; something that seemed to need protection. It was hard to guess if she was Indian or maybe bi-racial because of her creamy brown skin and gray-blue eyes. I didn't ask her, though, because she seemed to be intensely private. It was starting to bother me to think that Eric might ever be with Mia. But hell, maybe he already had.

The radio was playing the Doobie's "Blackwater"; a completely played out song in my opinion. When it finished and Manilow's "Mandy" came on, I changed the radio dial to an oldies station.

The second lyric of Janis Joplin singing "Me and Bobby McGee" wafted up through the marijuana smoke filled air. To my surprise, Mia began to sing a long and she wasn't half bad. I told her so and she smiled shyly.

"You cover this song, don't you?" she asked.

"We do," I replied. "But we don't have a girl singer; just Eric's sloppy effort to do the song justice. You should come on stage one night and sing it."

Mia lit up, and I saw for the first time how beautiful she really was.

"Could I?" she asked. Then her face clouded again. "I couldn't. I'd freak out."

"Well, it's just a local crowd." I told her. "No reason to be worried about what any of the swamp dwellers around here think. Could be fun; think about it." I'd used this line with girls many times before, but with Mia, I was pretty sure I meant it.

"Maybe I will," she said.

Eric and I had been playing in Savannah, New Orleans, Corpus Christi, and a few other towns in between for the past five years along with two other guys. We had a local following and the money was good. We hoped to get a record deal, but I wondered if Eric and I would be able to stand each other long enough to see that happen.

After a day of heat and pain in the ass tourists, I took Mia to *Jimmy's Bar* on Water Street. *Jimmy's* was a dive of a place owned by my friend, Sonny Domicco. Sonny was an Italian transplant from New York. He always wore slacks, dress shoes, a short-sleeved button down shirt, and a sweater vest despite the Savannah heat. It was as if he refused to accept that he lived in a semi-tropical climate instead of the year-round relative coolness of New York. I never knew whether anyone named Jimmy was associated with his bar, and something about Sonny told me not to ask.

The darkness inside the bar was a sharp contrast to the blistering sunlight outside, so it took a minute for my eyes to adjust. As I looked around, I once again took in the familiar wood paneled interior, the black leather chairs and barstools, the cheap wooden tables, and the cement floor. It was just after 3 p.m. in the afternoon, but already the place was filled with Sonny's regular customers. The air conditioning was a welcome relief from the heat of the day, and I relaxed almost as soon as the door closed behind us.

It was always good to come to *Jimmy's* where the jaded crowd of bookies and bikers who frequented the place didn't give a damn that I'd arrived. Local bar owners frequently asked me to play when they realized I was in the house. It was their way of getting some free entertainment for their customers. The attention was good for the band, but I still craved the privacy that *Jimmy's* gave me. As usual, barely anyone had looked my way when I walked in.

I was about to head over to the bar to get a drink when I felt Mia touch my arm.

"Where's the bathroom?" she asked.

"That way; in the back," I replied. I pointed the way past the bar where a crowd of men sat on bar stools and leaned over their drinks. Heavy clouds of cigarette smoke wafted through the air. The sound of Frank Sinatra's "Fly Me to the Moon" could be heard over clinking glasses and hushed conversations. Sonny only played singers like Frank, Dean, or Bobby but the rough and tumble crowd didn't seem to mind.

"Who's the half-breed?" a gruff voice from behind me asked.

"Well, I'd introduce you but she happens to be a nice girl," I replied. I slowly turned around to take in the full view of the owner of the voice. The man was a mammoth. He was at least six feet tall, heavily muscled, and he sported a full beard. He wore a black biker jacket and a red bandana.

"Don't get me wrong," he retorted. "I wouldn't kick her outta bed for having mutt blood."

"Well, I don't see why you would since piss and vinegar run through your veins."

Mountain laughed outright and clapped me on the shoulder. "Marty, you old son of a bitch! How've you been?"

"Good, Mountain, good. What brings you back to Savannah? They kick you out of Atlanta?"

"You bet they did! My old lady did anyway!" Mountain took a cigarette out of his jacket pocket and lit it.

Mountain was a fixture at *Jimmy's* when he was in town. He rode with a group of bikers and could always be counted upon to have the best weed. He often came out to the houseboat to crash. He usually stayed for a few days and then he'd disappear for months.

"Don't listen to this guy," Sonny said as he approached us waving his cigar. "Come and sit at my table and bring your lovely young lady."

"Well, she's in the ladies' right now. She won't know where I've gone off to." Sonny's table was really a booth in the back of the bar. A curtain was usually drawn around it to provide Sonny and his guests with privacy.

"Nonsense, Mike is watching for her. When she comes out he'll show her over."

Sonny wielded power quietly. There was something dangerous about him, but his hospitality was unfailing. We'd only just arrived at his bar, but he had organized an escort for Mia and he probably had my favorite drink waiting for me at his booth. As

Sonny ushered me away, Mountain took his cue and headed back to his biker buddies at the bar.

"Stop by the boat before you leave town again," I called after him. I wanted to get some weed before he took off again.

I followed Sonny to his booth and saw that my favorite drink, scotch on the rocks, was indeed waiting for me. An icy, clear drink that appeared to be a gin and tonic was sitting on the table as well. I was sure that it was for Mia. Sonny had anticipated that her feminine taste would want something along those lines, and I knew he'd replace it without hesitation if she didn't want it. Mia and I sat with Sonny for the rest of the afternoon, drinking and listening to his stories about New York. I was sure he told us the sanitized versions in order to protect the guilty. While he talked, customers and friends stopped by the booth intermittently to say hello to Sonny and pay their respect. At 6:30 p.m., Mia and I finally headed for home.

On the drive back we took a lot of back roads in order to avoid the police. In some spots, the edges of the road ran very close to swamps and marshes on both sides. I swore and swerved dangerously when a wet and bedraggled cat suddenly ran out in front of the car.

"We have to go back and get it!" Mia cried. "Someone must have dumped it out here. It will be alligator food if we don't rescue it!"

"Can't do it," I told her. "I'm deathly allergic to cats."

Chapter 3
Atlanta, Georgia, June, 2007

An African-American man dressed in sagging jeans and a wife-beater t-shirt was arguing heatedly with someone on his cellphone. I was parked next to him, but he didn't see me because my seat was laid back. I had arrived early for a doctor's appointment to get muscle relaxers for my back. It was killing me so instead of going inside, I thought I would stay inside my car and lay down. It would be better than sitting on one of Dr. Johnson's uncomfortable waiting room chairs. My plans were spoiled, however, because the man yelling outside my window was making my back seize up into a ferocious knot.

"Look, I am a **black** man; *a black man*." He began to laugh derisively. "I don't know what you think you're doin' messin' around with these little white boys...."

The person on the phone interrupted him and their argument escalated. He began to pace around as he listened to what they were saying. He walked out into the middle of the parking lot and blocked all the cars that were trying to pass. He self-centeredly ignored their horns and traffic began to back up.

The Darkness Behind the Door

Thoroughly annoyed, I thought of a hundred different ways that I could kill him. He didn't fit the profile exactly, but my temper was so bad from the pain that I didn't care. I would gladly have taken him out and certainly the people in the cars he blocked would have appreciated it, but it was the wrong time of year and too close to home. I only killed on Thanksgiving and Christmas when I was out of town. I had developed my routine to protect myself and I refused to stray from it. I'd had to resort to extreme measures once to avoid being arrested, and I didn't want to have to run again. Fortunately, the man finally left the parking lot and disappeared.

It was only 9:30 a.m., but the heat of the day was already seeping into my car. I lowered my windows and hoped that a breeze would blow through. As the minutes ticked by, I began to realize that a murder was taking place somewhere off to my left. There was an unsettled quality about a certain cluster of trees, and a baby bird was chirping a redundant call to its mother. Its chirping didn't vary one bit and the constant, repetitive sound was annoying. I looked around in exasperation and caught the silent, stealthy exit of a large hawk from the branches of the trees. Not even the leaves moved when he flew from his covered spot and no more chirping was heard. It had either flown off with the hatchling, or more likely eaten it right there in its nest. The baby bird had chirped the only sound it had developed in its young life while it was torn from limb to limb.

Inside the doctor's examination room, I put on a gown that opened to the back and waited for Dr. Johnson's nurse to check my vitals. I hated doctors, but I liked Kelly because she was good-looking, and I liked the muscle relaxers Dr. Johnson prescribed. The door to the exam room opened, but to my disappointment an older nurse walked in.

"Where's Kelly?" I asked.

"Kelly is off today, so I will be taking care of you," she said in a business-like tone. "What brings you in today, Mr. Jordanger?"

"Same old back injury," I replied. "Happened when I was in my twenties. Dr. Johnson knows all about it. I just need some meds, and I'll be fine."

"O.K. Shouldn't be a problem, but we'll want to get some X-rays first. Let's get your temperature and blood pressure and then X-ray will be in to take you down. After that, Dr. Johnson will be in to see you."

This nurse wasn't the looker Kelly was, but she seemed to know what she was doing and she said I could get my muscle relaxers. I nodded and allowed her to check my blood pressure and temperature, which were both normal. After the chilly trip to X-ray in the ass-viewing nightgown, I waited back in the exam room for Dr. Johnson. He made the whole ordeal worth it. He prescribed the muscle relaxers I'd come to get in the first place. As a child of the 70s, I didn't believe in living with pain that could be managed by narcotics.

Chapter 4
Hilton Head Island, October, 1975

The sound of water lapping against the side of the *Polargo* awakened me just before 6 a.m. It was still mostly dark, but I could see the female form of the woman who slept beside me. Mia's dark hair spilled around her shoulders. In the half light of the early morning her creamy skin was especially beautiful.

Mia was the daughter of a white mother and a black father whose grandparents were full-blooded Natchez Indians. I wasn't exactly sure what this made her by legal standards. In New Orleans, old society called women with a quarter of African blood "quadroons". If they had an eighth of African blood or less, they would have been called "griffons". They were renowned for their beauty and sought out by French gentlemen to be mistresses. The pla'cage contracts the gentlemen were required to enter into were binding and enforceable under the law. Looking at Mia, I felt a little guilty for thinking that she would have fetched a high price as a mistress way back when.

We'd just returned from visiting her family in New Orleans, Louisiana. They lived in a home on Conti Street in the French Quarter that had been built in the 1700s. It was built from red brick and featured a white portico with winding cement steps that descended on each side. Eight windows with black shutters, four upstairs and four downstairs, lined the façade. It was set back from the street and hidden from view by a tall, black wrought-iron fence.

Inside the home, a long hall extended all the way from the front door to the back and rooms led off from it on both sides. The formal living room, or parlor as Mia's family called it, was closest to the front door. It opened up into the formal dining room which also had a door off the main hall further down. Across the hall from the parlor was a library. Next to the library, was a less formal eating area and the kitchen. Ella, Mia's mother, showed me around and told me that the kitchen and informal dining area used to be a nursery and a master bedroom. The library was once a cigar room for men to retire to after parties. At the end of the hall was a staircase that led to the families' bedrooms upstairs.

Ella had me follow her out back to see the courtyard and a small set of apartments. In the center of the courtyard was a fountain, and behind it was the small apartment building. It sat on brick piers so that it was raised up from the ground. A short staircase led up to a wooden gallery. Narrow wooden railings provided support along the gallery walk-way just outside each apartment. Ella said slaves had lived in them once, but after slavery was abolished the apartments were given to the sons of the house so they could come and go as they pleased. We walked up the short staircase and went inside one of the rooms. It had no closet and contained only a wrought iron bed and a plain, brown rug. The floor and walls were made from the same thin, wooden planks that the porch was made from. Ella said she used most of the rooms for storage, but she rented two of them to tourists every year during Mardis Gras. We left the apartments and went to take a closer look at the wrought iron fence that lined the property. Ella pointed out the little shards of jagged glass and mirror that ran along the top of it and told me it was called a Romeo fence. She said that in the old days it was used to keep suitors from climbing over, but these days it kept the drunks from Bourbon Street out, rather than any would-be Romeos.

We went back inside the house and went into the parlor to look at some family photographs that were displayed on a large, oak table. Ella picked up one of Mia's younger brother, Ezra, and handed it to me. He was fourteen and very handsome in the same racially mixed way that Mia was. They looked almost identical except that Mia's eyes were more of a gray shade where his were bright blue. In another photo that looked like it had been taken at school, ten year old Cara was smiling brightly in her Catholic school uniform. She was more fair-skinned than either Mia or Ezra, but the family resemblance was definitely there.

Ella put her children's photos down and then solemnly picked up one of their father who had died six years ago. The picture showed a tall, dark, handsome man with kind eyes and a pleasant smile. Tears came into Ella's eyes as she looked at his picture. She stared at it for several minutes and seemed to forget my presence temporarily.

"He was a painter," she said at last. "Let me show you some of his work."

We left the parlor and went into the hall where two paintings of life on the streets of the New Orleans' French Quarter hung. In one painting, four young negro boys tap-danced in front of *Cafe' Dumonde* while on-lookers applauded. In the background, people sat at wrought iron tables and munched on beignets. The feeling of the painting was celebratory and chaotic. In the other painting, a winsome young woman stood in front of the Ursuline Convent. She looked lonely and lost, as though she'd come to the

Convent for help. *Bill Bouchard* was scrawled in the lower right corner of each painting.

"I don't know much about art," I told Ella. "But I like these."

She smiled at me. "Bill used to say that art is good if it moves you. Come on; let me show you a portrait he did of Mia."

I followed her into the library where a portrait of Mia hung over the fireplace. She looked like she was around ten, Cara's age. She was walking down a dock that stretched out over a murky body of water. Long reeds grew on both sides of the dock and a large, white shrimp boat floated behind her. She carried a fishing rod and a metal pail and she was laughing. From the position of the sun that was painted behind her, it appeared to be late in the day.

"How old was Mia when he painted this?" I asked.

"She was eleven years old. Bill painted it from a snapshot I took of her when we'd just come back from a fishing trip. She was really happy because she caught a big fish. You don't see it because Bill was holding it, but he wasn't in the shot."

"Where were you? Somewhere around here?" I asked.

"No, we were in Mobile visiting some of Bill's family. They were shrimpers. They used to have a seafood market on Dauphin Island Parkway. Bill painted two portraits of Mia from the pictures I took that day. The other one has Ezra in it. He was just five years old. It's hanging in Bill's gallery over on Royal Street."

Ella went over to a desk and opened one of its drawers. She pulled out a photo album and removed two photos.

"Here," she said as she handed me the photos. "These are the pictures I took. Here is the one of Mia by herself, and this is the one of her and Ezra together."

I took the photos from her to have a look. Mia and Ezra were exceptionally beautiful children. They both had creamy, brown skin and their hair was golden in the sun. Mia was still holding her fishing rod and the metal pail while Ezra pulled at his red and tan striped shirt.

"I'm surprised to see Mia so happy near the water," I said.

"Yes, that was *before*, you know. Ever since that incident on the ferry she's been scared of the water. Honestly, I'm shocked that she's willing to live on your houseboat."

"What incident?" I asked sharply.

A look of surprise came into Ella's eyes. "She didn't tell you?"

"No, she didn't. Tell me what happened." Ella looked uncomfortable, as though she felt she had said too much. "Please," I implored her.

"Well, O.K." she began, "but I'm only telling you because you should know how afraid she is of that houseboat. Please don't tell her I told you, though, because she doesn't like to talk about it. You see, when she was fifteen her father took her on the ferry that crosses the Mississippi River over to Algiers. They used to love to do that. There is some wonderful Spanish architecture over there that most people never see. Anyway, when the ferry completed its trip that day and the passengers were getting off, a little girl slipped on the gangway. She went over the side and ended up in the river. A lot of people went in after her, Bill included, but they couldn't save her."

"How old was the girl?" I asked.

"She was just a little thing, around five years old. The currents of the Mississippi sucked her down and took her down river. Her body wasn't found for nearly two weeks. Her poor mother never recovered. Mia never did, either."

Ella's story made me realize that Mia and I had both been shaped by events that happened when we were fifteen. I remembered the first night she came aboard the *Polargo*. She had been frightened by something in the water. She had said that it was pink.

"That's funny. Why did you say that?" Ella asked me.

"Why did I say what?" I replied, confused. I wasn't aware that I had said anything, not out loud anyway.

"You said the word *pink*. It's weird that you said it because Mia used to have nightmares about the little girl's pink dress. She said she remembered what the girl was wearing long after she forgot what the girl actually looked like. It haunted her for a long time."

It still does, I thought.

"Why don't you keep that photo of Mia?" Ella continued. "You can have it if you want."

"Are you sure?" I asked.

"Yes, of course. I can see how much you like it and I've got the painting. Here, I've got an envelope you can put it in."

She went back to the desk and got out a plain, white envelope. She handed it to me and I slid the photo inside. We went back out into the courtyard where Mia, Ezra, and Cara were drinking lemonade under an oak tree surrounded by palm fronds. The scent of magnolia was in the air. As I sat in the shade and drank lemonade with them, I realized I envied them because they loved each other so much. I wanted to be able to feel love like they did, instead of being so contemptuous of the human race and feeling empty all the time. I hadn't killed anyone since the pedophile at the community center, but the urge to do it was always there. To be like Mia and her family, I would have to let go of what happened to me when I was fifteen and forget my preoccupation with killing. As I watched Mia being affectionate and kind to Cara, I started to think about the kind of mother she would be. If I had children with her, maybe the darkness inside me would fade away. The longer I stayed with them, the more convinced I became that it would work. However, on the night I met Mia's grandparents my plan hit a snag and I came crashing back to reality.

We went to have dinner with them one evening because Ella said they wanted to meet me. I wondered why she seemed so nervous about it, but after a two hour drive on dirt roads that took us past swamps, levees, and the occasional shack, I forgot to ask. Just as I was beginning to think we would never get there, we finally pulled up in front a huge mansion that was surrounded by acres of moss-covered oak and magnolia trees.

As I turned into the driveway, Ella pointed at a body of water out in the distance. She said that in the old days, pirate ships had anchored there before the levees were built to protect the area from floods.

"Our people were Hugenots," Ella told me as we made our way up the driveway to the house. "We left France to escape religious persecution. My relatives settled here and built this place in 1830. It was a sugar plantation, but after the Civil War there wasn't anyone to work it. It's rumored that the family sold bootleg liquor to keep from going bankrupt. They got it from the pirates who used to dock out there where the levee is now."

Still playing tour guide, Ella told me that the house was built in the Greek revival style. Eight Doric columns the size of tree trunks lined both the front and back of the house. They supported the wide verandas that wound their way around the entire house at both the upstairs and downstairs levels. Four huge, double-hung windows spread across the façade. Ella said that when the windows were open, an adult could enter and exit through them with ease. They were made especially big, she said, to allow a breeze to blow through the house before air conditioning was in use.

The Darkness Behind the Door

We were greeted at the front door by an elderly black man who Mia told me was the butler. Harold had been with the family for years, she said, as had the cook and two maids. Inside the house, a long hall similar to the one in Ella's home extended through the entire downstairs. Rooms led off from it on opposite sides and a staircase at the end of it led upstairs. The style was similar to Ella's house, but the scale of her parents' house was overwhelming.

We followed Harold into a drawing room that had a high ceiling, gray walls, and rose-colored curtains. An ornate, gold leaf mirror hung over a marble fire-place. Before the fireplace was a mahogany framed sofa with silvery gray upholstery and claw feet. It sat across from two straight-back chairs. The only chair in the room that looked remotely comfortable was a beige armchair that sat by itself next to the fireplace. Before I could sit down, a young black woman came into the room and asked me what I wanted to drink. I requested a scotch and soda and she disappeared without asking anyone else what they wanted. Ezra and Cara each sat down on one of the straight-back chairs. I didn't want to be rude by sitting in the beige chair because it was so far from everyone, so I reluctantly followed Ella and Mia to the sofa. Soon the young woman reappeared with my scotch and soda, a Manhattan served in the appropriate glass for Ella, a glass of white wine for Mia, and lemonades for Ezra and Cara. After a few minutes, Mia's grandparents came into the room.

Mia's grandfather, Mr. Herbert Perry, was a well-preserved elderly man. He looked uncomfortable when Ella introduced us, but he shook my hand politely. Mia's grandmother, Mrs. Delphine Perry, said an icy hello to me and then took a seat in the beige armchair without speaking to anyone else. She lit a cigarette and began to smoke as though she was in a trance. She took long drags followed by slow, delicate exhales and watched her hands intently as they flicked ashes into a crystal ashtray. I immediately felt under-dressed in my slacks and a shirt with no tie because Mr. Perry was dressed in a pin-striped, seer sucker suit and Mrs. Perry wore an elegant black dress. Her gray hair was twisted into a chignon. The young woman who had served drinks to us brought a martini to Mrs. Perry and a drink that looked like another scotch and soda to Mr. Perry. When I looked around I noticed that Mia was drinking her wine rather quickly and Ella looked uncomfortable, too.

"Ella tells me you're a musician," Mr. Perry said. "What instrument do you play?"

"The guitar," I replied, "and I sing a little, too. Mostly back-up vocals, but I sing lead on a couple of songs we do."

"Oh, how interesting," he said flatly. He didn't look like he thought it was interesting at all. Behind him, Mrs. Perry looked bored.

"Ella told me you're in a band," he continued. "What was the name of it?"

"The Henley-McCloud Band," I replied.

"Where do you play?" Mr. Perry asked in a valiant attempt to keep the conversation going.

"All along the Gulf Coast," I told him. "We've played in New Orleans many times before, but I never experienced it the way I am now with Mia to show me around." I smiled at Mia. She looked down self-consciously and then looked back at me and gave me a nervous smile.

"Do you perform your own material?' he asked.

Mr. Perry's question made the color rise in the back of my neck. It reminded me of the fight I had with Eric just before I left for New Orleans. I wanted to make a tape with a record producer I knew in Corpus Christie, Texas, but Eric wanted to keep things the way they were. He was happy doing the same old covers because the money was good. He kept saying we weren't ready to cut a record, but I knew he didn't want to because he didn't trust me. He had no intention of doing business with a producer I introduced him to. Just as I was about to answer Mr. Perry's question, the young woman who was serving drinks handed me my second scotch and soda. One of us tipped the glass a little and some of it spilled onto my shirt. I stood up quickly as I felt the cold liquid seep through to my skin.

"Lydia!" Mrs. Perry hissed.

Lydia stepped back from me like a scolded child. She quickly took a paper napkin from the silver tray she carried and began to briskly wipe my shirt with it.

"Forget the stupid shirt, Lydia!" Mrs. Perry bellowed. "Make sure you didn't get any on the sofa or the rug!"

Lydia looked at the sofa and then at the rug. "I don't see any stains, ma'am," she said.

"Look more closely. Make **sure**, Lydia!" Mrs. Perry instructed from her armchair. I moved out of the way so Lydia could inspect the place where I'd been sitting.

"I don't see any stains, ma'am," Lydia repeated.

"I think it only got on my shirt," I said. "No harm done." I smiled at Lydia. Mrs. Perry glared at me.

"Go and see about dinner," Mr. Perry told Lydia curtly.

I watched Lydia's exit until a portrait of a man caught my attention. His face seemed to change as I looked at it.

"That's an unusual portrait," I said. "May I ask who that is?"

Mr. Perry turned and regarded the portrait.

"Yes, certainly," he said. "That is a portrait of both my grandfather **and** my great-grandfather. You see, if you move around the room so you can view the painting from different angles, you will see the face of one man or the other. Paintings like this used to be done as a sign of great respect. They were great men. They did a lot for this family."

There was an uncomfortable pause and then Mrs. Perry put her martini down on the table next to her chair. She smoothed her hair and looked over at me.

"Would you like a tour of the house?" she asked.

She spoke in a soft, refined southern accent, but her face was dead-pan. I got the distinct impression that she didn't really want to give me a tour. Maybe someone had made a deal with her, but in exchange for what, I didn't know.

"Sure, I would love to see the house," I answered.

Mrs. Perry reluctantly crushed out her cigarette and smoothed her hair again. "Will it just be you?" she asked.

"Mia, you go with Marty and Delphine," Ella said. "I'll stay here with Cara and Ezra."

"No, Mommy, please!" Cara pleaded. "I want to go with them! I want to see Papa's big house!" She sat up on the edge of her chair and pursed her lips, but Ezra only shrugged.

"No, Cara, you've seen it before," Ella told her.

The under-current of tension I thought I sensed seemed to have escalated into an electrical storm. There was obviously something unpleasant and unsaid going on between Ella and her parents.

Mr. Perry stared at the bottom of his highball. "They can go, Ella," he said. "Mia can keep an eye on them."

Ella didn't look convinced but she said, "O.K., children, you can go, but don't touch anything."

"I'll stay here with you, Mama," Ezra said.

Mia, Cara, and I followed Mrs. Perry out of the drawing room and went into the grand hall. An eighteen lamp chandelier cast a warm glow over us from where it hung from the high ceiling.

Mrs. Perry walked over to a long sofa that had a low back and worn, gold cushions.

"This piece has been in my family for years," she said. "You see this crown with the leaf here?"

She ran her hand over a gold cushion, and I saw the faded black crown and leaf design for the first time.

"This is my family's crest," she continued. "We were in the teak wood manufacturing business. The sofa's frame is made from teak." She paused and looked at me through narrowed eyes. "My family used this sofa for business associates and guests who weren't close to the family. They would have waited on it out here in the hall until a family member allowed them to come further inside the house."

The cold way she looked at me seemed to say that she thought I should have been kept waiting there on the sofa instead of being allowed to socialize in the drawing room. I was beginning to get the picture that she didn't like me. Maybe that was the reason for all the tension. But if that was the case, why had we come? We left the hall and went into a formal living room. The walls were painted turquoise and heavy, gold curtains hung over the windows. Every piece of furniture in the room was detailed and ornate.

"These chairs are French Heppelwhite," she explained blandly, "and the sofa is from the Louis XV period."

She could have been speaking to school children. Her tone was dry and forced as though she thought her words were wasted on us. We left the formal living room and went into a smaller room next door.

"This is a sitting room for Herbert and me. We don't have guests in here very often."

The furniture in this room was more modern. A stream-lined, white sofa was accented by two golden teak end-tables and a matching coffee table. Built-in bookshelves lined the walls next to yet another fireplace and the ceiling was lower. Through double French doors I spotted a beautiful courtyard outside, but Mrs. Perry didn't offer to show it to us.

"Let's head upstairs," she said coldly. "You will see the dining room at dinner and I don't think we should go into the kitchen and disturb Mittie while she's cooking."

I was getting tired of Mrs. Perry's superior attitude, but I went on with the tour because I didn't want to embarrass Ella. We followed Mrs. Perry up a winding, highly polished staircase that creaked underneath our feet. When we reached the second floor, she led us into a room that was dark and masculine. She turned on a lamp that sat on a massive mahogany desk and soft light filled the room.

"This is Herbert's study. I had the walls paneled in teak on our second anniversary," she said as she pointed to one of the carved wood panels.

Two framed photographs of Mr. and Mrs. Perry at younger ages sat on a bookcase next to a crystal decanter. In one photo, Mrs. Perry stood next to an orange tree while she smoked a cigarette. In the other photo, both Mr. and Mrs. Perry were seated at a long table with eight other people. Everyone was smiling, smoking, and drinking. We left the study and went into a guest bedroom that contained a mahogany, four-post bed. Finally, we went into the last room on the tour. It was painted light blue and mint green drapes hung over the windows. There wasn't a lot of furniture in it except for a dilapidated sofa and a small, outdated television set that sat on a utilitarian, metal rolling cart. Behind the sofa was a table on which several small Victorian-era figurines were placed.

The Darkness Behind the Door

"This is the upstairs sitting room," Mrs. Perry said as she leaned against the doorway behind us. "Herbert and I just roll that cart around if one of us wants to watch T.V."

She straightened herself up and smoothed her hair again. "Well, that's it except for the master bedroom, but you can't expect me to show you that!" she snapped.

We started to follow her back downstairs when Cara stumbled and bumped the sofa table. She sent one of the delicate looking Victorian figurines flying across the room. She and Mia both looked panic-stricken as Mrs. Perry went to retrieve it from where it landed on the floor next to the metal rolling cart.

"Cara, your mother told you to be careful and not touch anything, didn't she?" Mrs. Perry asked as she walked over to Cara with the figurine in her hand. Her eyes were deadly. She seemed to have grown six inches in height. She radiated hatred at Cara, who seemed to shrink before my eyes.

"Yes, ma'am," Cara replied in a shaky, little voice. She looked like she was about to burst into tears.

"These figurines are from the Victorian Age. They are expensive, personal items that your grandfather and I have collected over the years. They cannot be replaced."

"Yes, ma'am," Cara said again as the tears she had tried to hold back began to slide down her cheeks.

"If you'd been brought up correctly, you would have more respect for other people's things," Mrs. Perry continued.

Mia put her arm around Cara. "It was an accident," she said.

"Accident or not, the things in this house cannot be replaced," Mrs. Perry repeated angrily.

"That's what insurance is for," I interrupted. "File a claim."

I returned Mrs. Perry's angry gaze with a look of warning. I wanted to snatch the damned figurine from her hand and then take the sofa table Cara bumped and break it over her head.

"Let's go back downstairs," Mrs. Perry sniffed.

Mia held Cara's hand as we descended the stairs. Mrs. Perry went back into the drawing room, but Mia stopped Cara before she followed her. She placed her hand on Cara's shoulder and then gently tilted her face upward so she could look directly in her eyes.

"Don't worry about it, Cara," she told her. "You didn't break it."

"I didn't mean to hit the table," Cara said sadly.

"I know, sweetie. Listen, one less figurine in this house wouldn't hurt anyone. Don't be sad about it anymore, O.K.? I bet Mittie made a special dessert just for you."

Cara smiled at her and then the three of us walked into the drawing room. Ella immediately saw that something was wrong, but Mia caught her eye and softly shook her head. Mrs. Perry was back in her beige chair again, smoking her cigarette and drinking her martini. After a few minutes, she took her cigarette and the martini and quietly left the room. Mr. Perry didn't comment on her leaving.

"Go and see if dinner is served," he said to Lydia.

She nodded and disappeared through a heavy swinging door at the far end of the drawing room. After a moment, she reappeared and announced that dinner was served. We each gingerly made our way to the dining room where a long table was elaborately set with food.

"Will we wait for Mrs. Perry?" I asked.

"No, she isn't feeling well so we will eat without her," he replied. I wondered when this bit of information had passed between them.

The dinner was a traditional New Orleans style meal. Turtle soup was followed by a shrimp remoulade salad, followed by a main course of snapper and sweet potatoes, after which came crème brulee and café aulait. The food was delicious but the conversation was strained. I was glad that the scotch kept coming. I was working on my fourth drink and needed to go to the bathroom but Mrs. Perry had neglected to point one out on the tour.

Where's the closest bathroom?" I whispered to Mia.

"Go out into the hall and take a right," she whispered back. "Go past the downstairs sitting room and it's the next door on the left."

"Excuse me for a moment," I said to everyone as I slid my chair backward. I got up and left the table.

When I walked into the hall, I smelled cigarette smoke coming from the sitting room. I walked over to the open doorway and saw Mrs. Perry sitting on the white, stream-lined sofa with her legs tucked underneath her. She didn't see me because she was reading a book, but I noticed that she didn't look sick. A fresh martini was sitting on the coffee table in front of her and she was smoking another cigarette. I wondered if she had gotten out of eating dinner with us by agreeing to give us a tour. Without saying anything to her, I walked past the doorway and found the bathroom further down the hall. Back at the dinner table, I didn't mention what I had seen. Soon after dessert was finished, Ella thankfully announced that it was time to head home. I shook Mr. Perry's hand and thanked him for his hospitality.

"Wonderful meeting you, my boy," he replied.

I drove back toward the French Quarter through the black Louisiana night. The car's headlights lit a small path through the fog that had begun to set in. My eyes felt heavy as I looked at the rutted road ahead of me. Mia dozed beside me. Her head was on my shoulder, and her long, curly hair tickled my arm. I looked in the rear-view mirror and saw that both Cara and Ezra were asleep as well. Only Ella and I were awake. She smiled at me in the mirror and brushed some hair from Cara's sleeping face.

"It's beautiful out here, isn't it?" she asked.

"Yes," I replied, "And strange."

"You mean that tonight was strange, don't you?" she asked. She wore a light smile on her face.

"Well, I enjoyed myself," I lied. "Your parents have a beautiful home. I guess your mother wasn't feeling well after she gave us the tour."

"She isn't my mother," Ella replied sharply.

"She isn't?" I asked. "I'm sorry. I didn't know."

"Of course you didn't know. How could you? I didn't mention it because Dad doesn't like for me to talk about it. It's important to him that we **try** to be a family. You see, Delphine is my stepmother."

"Is her family in the teak manufacturing business?" I asked. I was trying to keep the conversation light because I could see that Ella was starting to get upset.

"Yes, they were at one time. She's not from New Orleans, though. Her family is from California. She didn't move into the house until Dad married her, but later on she did some of the rooms in teak to put her mark on them. I was seventeen when they got married and we never really got along."

"Oh," I replied. I didn't know what else to say. I could only imagine what it must have been like to grow up with someone like Mrs. Perry around.

"That house has been in my family since the 1800s but when Dad dies he's leaving it to Delphine," Ella said bitterly. "And when she dies she will most certainly leave it to her kids. She has a son in California and a daughter in Texas. The only way that house will stay in the Perry family is if Delphine dies before Dad does."

"I see," I replied. I could feel my murderous impulses rising up again. If I killed Mrs. Perry, I could help Ella and insure that she, Mia, Ezra, and Cara inherited their family home.

"It's my punishment for marrying Bill because he was black," Ella continued. "Dad and I didn't speak for nearly sixteen years after I married him, but we've tried to put the pieces back together. It's been hard, though. Mia, Ezra, and Cara have suffered because of it."

Oh," I said again. I remembered how harsh Mrs. Perry had been with Cara. There was obviously more behind her anger than a broken figurine.

"Mia had it the hardest because she was the first child. The family was at war when she was little. She has been very hurt, but she doesn't hold any grudges. She's a special person, but she's fragile. You have to watch out for her, Marty. You know that, don't you?"

"I know," I said.

My hope of becoming a person who was filled with love like Mia and her family was quickly slipping away. But it was O.K., because this time, the murderous hatred I felt was in defense of the people I loved. Mrs. Perry was a cruel, bigoted woman who had tortured Ella, Mia, Ezra, and Cara and threatened their inheritance. They would be better off if she was dead. Maybe one day, Mrs. Perry and I would meet again.

Chapter 5
Atlanta, Georgia, September, 2007

"Mitch, I can't believe this is what my career has come to," Lauren said as she set the birthday cake down on the small dining table in the company break room. To her credit, she had put a yellow plastic table cloth and a vase of flowers beside the cake to "up the festivity factor of this sad little occasion" she'd said.

"Don't get me wrong," she continued. "I believe that the company should acknowledge employee birthdays. It's just that the tired old office birthday party is about as pathetic as festive shirt day. Who needs a reminder that we cubicle rats have so little to look forward to?"

Just then Drexler stuck his head into the kitchen. "Ummmm.....caaaakke! When do we eat?"

I could tell Lauren was doing her best not to roll her eyes. "2 p.m.," she said. She even managed a small smile.

"I'll be here to get my two pieces!" Drexler said and disappeared.

Lauren turned to me and lowered her voice. "I think he has Asperger's Syndrome."

"Really, why?" I asked.

Experience had taught me that Lauren often had insight into such things. She was a former VP of Operations for a lender that had gone bust in the economic downturn of 2006. Now she functioned as the Office Administrator/Facilities Coordinator/Jr. Human Resources rep at *Wilson's Security Systems*, the small software company where we both worked. She had noticed things about our co-workers that had proven to be true several times before, so I stayed on my toes when I was around her. I didn't want her figuring out any of my secrets, after all.

"Well, he speaks in a mechanical sort of way," she said. "And, he can't come through the front door without being as distracted as a moth by a light bulb when the sensors go off. He stands and listens to the damn things as if he's in a trance. Mark would never put up with incompetence so I have to figure that he's good at his job, but then his work as a computer programmer would probably suit someone with Aspergers."

Bert stuck his head in the kitchen doorway. "What kind of cake did you get, Lauren?"

"Chocolate with white icing," she replied.

"Not chocolate with chocolate icing? Too bad."

"Right, I know that's your favorite, but I went with what Nikki wanted. It's her birthday, after all."

"Oh, well. What time do we eat?" he asked.

"2 p.m. You should have an invitation on your office calendar."

Bert nodded and sort of skipped off in his usual hyper manner.

Lauren turned to me. "Dear God, Mitch, give me a Xanax before there's blood all over that damned cake! The fact that I plan office birthday parties for a living now is just too depressing!"

A couple of hours later, Lauren and I went to lunch at our favorite middle-eastern restaurant that was near the office. Inside the restaurant, our regular waiter waved us over to our usual booth. He knew what we wanted before we ordered because we always had the same thing, chicken kabobs with rice and a side order of hummus with pita bread. Lauren had been quiet on the drive over and she still didn't say much after we sat down. When Sunil brought the lentil soup that always came before the entrée she asked him to bring her a glass of white wine. When he left the table to get it for her from the bar, I waited expectantly for her to tell me what was bothering her.

"What?" she asked defensively when she saw me looking at her. "You don't approve of me having a glass of wine at lunch? Honestly, Mitch, I could do that job in my sleep."

"It's not that," I told her. "It's just that you've been kind of quiet and now you're having wine." I decided not to mention that she'd already gotten a Xanax from me earlier that day. "What's going on, Lauren? I can tell that something is wrong."

"I don't want to talk about it," she said dismissively. When Sunil arrived with the glass of wine she took it from him and immediately started drinking.

I decided not to push it. Lauren knew her own mind and if she didn't want to talk about it then I would respect her wishes. I didn't like that she wouldn't confide in me though, because it signaled that I couldn't confide in her. I wanted to tell her my secrets, but right then it seemed like I never would. I studied her subtly while we ate so she wouldn't notice what I was doing. Her stylish dress and expensive jewelry belied her current circumstances at *Wilson's Security Systems*. She used to make a lot of money as the Vice President of an investment bank, but she had lost her job after the economy crashed. I knew she was divorced and had a nine year old daughter to support. She never talked about it, but I suspected that she was having serious financial problems.

As usual, I reached for the check when Sunil brought it over before she had a chance to grab it.

"I'll get this," I said.

"O.K., but I'll get it next time," she replied.

She was still quiet as she drove us back to the office. I glanced over at her profile and wished that she would talk to me. When she made a left, bright sunlight scattered across her face in droplets. I was sure I saw a bruise on her cheek. It looked like it had carefully been covered with make-up.

"Lauren," I said seriously. "If you need help, please tell me."

She gave me a look that told me she knew I had seen the bruise.

"Thank you," she said, "but I'm fine."

Someone was hurting her and I wanted to know who it was. More than that, I wanted make sure that it never happened again.

"Really, Lauren, you don't know it, but I could help you more than you realize."

"I appreciate that, but I don't need any help," she replied flatly.

I wasn't going to let it go. "We both know what I saw, Lauren. Why are you pretending that you don't need help? Someone did that to you. You know it and I know it-"

Lauren made a hard right and angrily pulled over onto the shoulder of the road. When she did it, she cut off the driver who was in the next lane. He laid on his horn and flipped us off as he passed, but Lauren ignored him. She turned to me with her eyes blazing.

"So what? You saw it! Well, congratulations!" She vigorously rubbed at the make-up that covered the bruise and revealed a huge black and blue spot. "You see this and you think I need rescuing, is that it? Well, I don't need you to rescue me. Do me a favor, Mitch, and let me handle my own problems!"

Karen Oliver

Maybe it was her pride or maybe she was protecting someone, but it felt like the distance between us was wider than ever. How could I tell her any of my secrets if she wouldn't tell me any of hers? I thought I might have found the one person who could handle the truth about me, but she was unwilling to let me in.

Chapter 6
Corpus Christie, Texas, June, 1976

The Henley-McCloud Band was finishing its last set at *The Lighthouse*. Located in the marina of downtown Corpus Christie, TX, the old lighthouse formerly functioned as the real thing for ships out in the Gulf of Mexico. In the 1950s, it had been converted to a restaurant and bar. The area we played in had been built as an addition to the older structure. The sound stage we occupied was built over the bar so customers had a good view of the band as we played and also of the bartenders who hustled to sling drinks all night. The joint was a regular stop on our circuit and we knew the owner, Brian, very well. He was an ugly man with ruddy skin, piercing blue eyes, and somehow he had too many teeth for his mouth. He'd managed the place for years before graduating to owner when he married the older widow whose late husband left her the place. He was beefy, bald, and spoke with a strong Boston accent; truly a rarity in Texas. He ran *The Lighthouse* with a heavy hand and the staff hated him, but the tips were excellent because the place was full almost every night.

Eric, Dave, Vince, and I had agreed that we would close with a cover of the Stones "Honky Tonk Woman," and do only one song for an encore. We'd leave the stage and return to do Skynnerd's "Give Me Three Steps" and that would be it. I was itching to get upstairs to the lines of coke I knew were waiting in the restaurant offices. The lines had been laid out for us by Officer Cisco Rodriguez, another friend and an esteemed member of local law enforcement no less. His afternoon bust had been our gain all night.

Mia sat at a table near the stage with Jill and Jeri. Jill was with our crazy drummer, Dave, who looked like a heavy version of the Marlboro man. They had never married, but they had a five year old daughter named Eve. Jeri was a dark-eyed heroin addict who Eric saw whenever he was in Corpus. I had fought with him about Jeri at band practice earlier that day. I'd told him that if he was graduating to needles, he was out of the band. We weren't successful enough for him to overdose yet. He'd retorted with an accusation that I was stealing money from the band, and I, with my typical concern for his feelings, had told him to go to hell.

At last, we finished the set and I packed up my guitar. Mia and I headed upstairs to the office, did a few lines, and sat around bullshitting a while before we decided to leave. We walked outside, and in my heightened state of awareness I was keenly tuned in to the sound of the gravel parking lot crunching under my feet. We walked in moonlight past parked vehicles until we reached my bike.

I got on and fired up the engine and Mia slid on behind me. My guitar was strapped across her body, so it prevented me from feeling her breasts against my back. I drove slowly under fluorescent lights that were outshone by the full moon. Old, brown palm trees swayed gently in the yards of the bungalow-style houses that we passed. We left the side road and got onto Highway 358 to head to South Padre Island. There was barely any traffic on the small highway that led away from the rowdy bars of downtown Corpus Christi toward South Padre's deserted beaches. I was ready to get away from the crowds and listen to the sound of big waves rolling in from the night sea.

When we reached our camping spot I pulled right up to the pop-up tent that Mia and I were going to sleep in. Driving on the beach was legal in Corpus. It didn't make for the most beautiful sand, but it was great to be able to go to parties on the beach where cars parked in row after row. South Padre's sand was coarse and dark brown, and the ocean was opaque, gray, and salty. One slap from a wave could easily leave a salt burn. Jelly Fish and sharks were numerous and oil pumping stations were visible from the shore. What the beaches lacked in beauty, they made up for with frequent parties, regular live music shows, and sand-sculpting contests. Elaborately carved dolphins, mermaids, and castles were frequent sights along the shoreline. Sailing regattas, whale watching, and skate boarding were also part of the laid-back scene where no one had a serious job and no one was much interested in getting one.

It was nearly 2 a.m. when we arrived at the beach. The wind and the sound of crashing waves felt good. I started a fire and Mia brought out some weed and beer so we could come down from all the coke. We sat by the fire and looked out at the water for a while before Dave and Jill showed up with Eve, who was fast asleep. Jill put Eve in their tent and then joined us in front of the campfire. Eventually, Vince, our bass player, arrived with a double-D'd waitress from *The Lighthouse* who'd given me the eye all night. There was no sign of Eric or Jeri. It looked like he was going to stay in her apartment again rather than join us on the beach. He was probably still pissed at me because of the fight we had, but I didn't care. The starlit night and the ocean were beautiful. It was his loss if he didn't want to join us. Before long I felt

The Darkness Behind the Door

Mia tug on my arm to get me to follow her to our tent for a restful sleep.

Mia walked ahead of me on the gangway as we prepared to enter the old pirate ship. Its massive, wooden structure rocked and creaked in the water. About halfway across the small bridge with rope railings, Mia stopped and pointed down toward the sea water. Her back was to me, and her arm pointed rigidly away from her side though her head and body remained strangely erect and shipward facing. I heard something struggling in the water so I came up behind her to have a look.

A gull with a broken wing struggled desperately to stay afloat in the deep sliver of water that separated the ship and the dock.

"We have to save him," she said quietly.

"Mia," I said to her back, "those things are rats with wings. They carry disease. Better let nature take its course."

Suddenly, I was much further away from her than I had been when I stood behind her on the gang-way. She faced me from where she still stood on the bridge, and she held the gull high above her head. Her gray-blue eyes blazed with anger and determination. In one graceful, sickening move, she sliced the blade across the gull's neck. Red blood spurted into her hair and across her face, and then she threw the gull directly at me. It landed at my feet and turned immediately into a live rat that scampered back toward the ship across the gangway.

In complete shock, I stood speechless before Mia.

"The blood on our hands will follow us wherever we go," she said.

I awoke with a start inside the nylon tent to find myself completely twisted up in the sleeping bag and blankets Mia and I had shared. I blinked hard and realized Mia wasn't lying beside me. I had no idea what time it was but the heat of the day was already seeping in and sweat dripped down my forehead. I pushed my damp hair away from my face and tried to gather my wits. The dream I'd just awakened from had been very unsettling. I wanted to see Mia and experience her sweet personality to put things back in perspective. I heard waves rolling gently in the morning tide, but then I heard another sound as well. It was the sound of someone crying. I quickly unzipped the tent and peered out into the sunshine. It was far too bright for someone who'd consumed the amount of drugs and alcohol that I had last night. My eyes adjusted and I saw that Jill was the one who was crying. She sat clutching her knees as she rocked back and forth in front of the smoldering campfire. Mia was sitting beside her but neither Dave, Vince, nor the waitress were anywhere in sight. Mia must have felt me watching them because she looked over at me. She said something to Jill, patted her arm, and then came over.

"Evie is missing," she said, her eyes close to tears.

"What? Where is everyone?" I asked, unable to grasp what I was hearing.

"Dave, Vince, and Katrina are out looking for Eve. Jill and I walked up and down the beach already but we didn't see her. Everyone is really worried. Jill said she woke up and Eve wasn't there. We can't imagine what's happened. Maybe she got up in the night to use the bathroom or something…." Her voice trailed off as if she couldn't bear to say anything more. I crawled out of the tent with only my shorts on and went over to where Jill sat nearly incoherent with grief.

"Look, Jill, she's got to be around here somewhere. Let's you, me, and Mia look for her down the beach again."

She nodded without looking at me.

"Better yet," I said when I considered that Eve might return to camp and find no one there, "you stay here in case Eve comes back. Mia will search the sand dunes, and I'll go down the beach. We'll go as far as we have to until we find her, I promise."

Jill nodded and continued rocking where she sat on the brown sand. Mia and I looked at each other, not sure if we should leave her, but it made more sense to aid in the search than to console the grieving mother. There would be plenty of time for that if Eve was never found. Mia and I began our walk beside the crashing waves that ran under our feet and I felt the undertow. The ocean had become a taunting enemy. Each wave seemed to say, "I could have her, and you'll never know for sure." In desperation, I asked everyone I met if they'd seen a five year old girl with white- blonde hair. I couldn't believe that she was gone. We'd all been so high last night that we never even knew she'd left or been taken. I took Mia's hand in mine and noticed that it was shaking. I was sure she felt like the nightmare she experienced when she was fifteen was happening all over again. Another little girl was missing and possibly drowned.

"We better split up," she said. "We can cover more ground that way."

I nodded, worried about how she was feeling. I reluctantly let go of her hand and watched her as she walked toward a group of people who were lounging on towels to ask them if they'd seen Eve. We didn't have a photo, of course, and even though people were sympathetic, drunks on a beach weren't exactly a reassuring bunch when it came to finding a lost little girl. I kept going for an undetermined time, and my skin was burning in the sun. I asked everyone who played Frisbee with their dogs, lounged in the sun, or bathed in the shallow ocean water if they'd seen the missing five year old.

Eventually, I came upon the deep intra-coastal water-way where ships passed through the channel. The water was especially dark and deep. A pelican that looked to be almost my height stood a lonely vigil on the other side of the channel. The bird and I stared at each other for some time.

For the hell of it, I yelled, "Seen a little girl around here?"

He didn't like my yelling, and he flew a slow, heavy flight just a bit further away from me. He came to rest in front of a bridge that ran from one side of the channel to the other. I had no logical reason to be, but I was extremely pissed at this bird. I jogged lightly down my side of the channel so that I stood directly across from him again. He flapped his massive wings to show me he could hold his own, and I felt ashamed for being such a bastard to this bird that only wanted solitude. I had given up on finding Evie, but I decided to cross the bridge before I went back.

I walked up the short flight of cement steps and paused to stare down at the black water below. It was all too easy to imagine Evie floating face down with her blonde hair and white dress splayed around her. God, it just couldn't be true. Eve couldn't be here in the depths or somewhere out at sea with sharks keeping her company. I sat for some time on the steps of the bridge. My fair Irish skin had burned so deeply that it was beginning to turn brown.

As I sat there not knowing if Eve was alive or dead, I suddenly felt intensely aware of my own mortality. The lonely pelican, the bridge, and the deep water all seemed like perfect symbols of death. I had killed a man so maybe this was the kind of after-life I was going to have. When I died, maybe something as silent as the pelican was going to escort me across a bridge that stretched out over a dark abyss but led to nowhere. There I would stay, completely and utterly alone. I suddenly wanted to see Mia more than ever. I started back to camp at a pace that was dangerously fast since I hadn't had any water except for what I mixed with my scotch last night. Luckily, I came upon two guys who recognized me from last night's performance at *The Lighthouse*. They hooked me up with a couple of beers.

"Man!" One of the long-haired hippies remarked, "You look like you've been walking for days! You sure you're O.K., man?"

I told them I was fine and asked if they'd seen Eve, but they hadn't. Exhausted and dehydrated, I stayed to smoke a joint with them and drank a couple more beers. The sun was beginning to set when I started walking again. After a while, I saw our tents and a campfire burning in the distance. When I got closer I saw that Dave, Mia, Eric, and Jeri were sitting around the campfire. Jill, Evie, Vince, and Katrina were nowhere to be seen. Eric saw me before anyone else did.

"Hey, old man!" he yelled. He had evidently forgotten about the argument we had yesterday.

Mia followed his voice and then ran to meet me.

"Evie just walked right up to camp about three hours ago," she said excitedly. "She had been playing with some kids on the beach in the other direction from where you and I were looking. Jill and I went that way earlier, but somehow we missed her."

I could have passed out with relief.

"That's great," I said. I glanced over at Dave who was shakily drinking Jack Daniels straight from the bottle. "Where are Jill and Eve now?" I asked.

"Vince and Katrina drove them to Jill's sister's house. Jill is coming back to camp out, but they don't want to take a chance with Eve out here again."

I knew then why Dave was downing Jack Daniels like it was water. Delaney didn't like Dave. She and Jill were identical twin sisters with personalities that were as different as night and day. They were both small-framed and had white-blonde hair that flowed all the way down to their tiny waists, but the similarity stopped there. Laney was the stressed out, straight-arrow version of Jill who was the most laid-back, easy-going hippie I had ever met. Laney used to be cool before her husband died in a car accident in which both he and the other driver were drunk. Ever since then Laney had become something of a repressed bitch.

Both Dave and Jill were born and raised in Corpus Christie so their families knew each other and they didn't get along. The fact that Jill had chosen to live in a common-law marriage and have a child with Dave, a wild, hard-partying drummer who was always on the road, definitely didn't sit well with them.

I walked over to Dave and clapped him on the back. "Glad everything's O.K., man," I told him.

He nodded. "Thanks for looking for her," he said.

Mia escorted me to the tent, got me some water, and rubbed cool aloe on my back. I fell asleep to the feeling of her soft hands smoothing cool liquid onto my burning flesh and knew no more.

Chapter 7
Atlanta, Georgia, October, 2007

Ralphie was dead. Twelve years of companionship but now he was gone; a living entity no more. I found him when I came home from the record store for lunch. At first he appeared to be sleeping, but when I got closer I saw that he was stiff and lying in a pool of his own excrement. I was glad that the other cats had left him alone. His body appeared undisturbed. I grabbed an old towel from the garage that we used to wash our cars with and put on a pair of rubber gloves. I carefully wrapped him in the towel because his dander could cause my throat to swell and stop me from breathing. The fact that I was deathly allergic to cats never registered with Melanie as a reason that we shouldn't take in strays. We had adopted a total of ten cats, now nine remained after the loss of Ralphie. I picked him up carefully, grabbed a shovel, and went out back to dig his grave.

He'd been a good cat; one of the more likeable ones in the group. He was even tempered and kept his distance from me, and he had been good at catching rodents. I appreciated that since I kept a guitar, a drum set, and some stage speakers in the shed in the backyard. He was one of Melanie's favorites, so I knew she was going to take his passing hard. I dug his grave near a Crape Myrtle tree in our back yard, lowered him down with the shovel, and covered him up with the loose dirt I'd unearthed. I then placed a large rock on top of his grave so Melanie could visit when she got home. The other cats stayed away while I performed my somber duty. Only Otto drifted by to see what was going on. I wasn't worried about them digging him up. I didn't think cats dug things up like dogs did, and I had buried him pretty deep.

I drove back to the *Night Owl* and finished the rest of the day uneventfully. At 6 p.m. Kenny, a band-member who gave music lessons at my record store, was finishing up a guitar lesson with Anna, an awkwardly beautiful girl of thirteen. She was of mixed ethnicity. She had curly brown hair, creamy skin, and blue-gray eyes. She was shy and sweet. She hadn't bloomed yet but when she did, she was going to be a knock-out. Seeing her was always bitter-sweet because she reminded me of Mia.

The sound of beginner's chords being played on a guitar stopped and Kenny walked out from the back of the shop with Anna trailing behind. She stood up straight, but she always kept her head down in a demure sort of way.

"How'd it go this evening, Anna?" I asked with a big smile to put her at ease. "Kenny's not wasting your time, is he?"

She smiled shyly and said very earnestly, "No, he's not wasting my time, Mr. Jordanger."

"Good, because we wouldn't want him goofing off back there."

A look of concern came over her young face. She seemed to be worried that Kenny really was in trouble.

"I'm just kidding, Anna. Kenny's a good teacher, isn't he?"

She immediately brightened; another quality of hers that made me think of Mia.

"Oh, yes, Mr. Jordanger. My mom says I'm getting real good."

"Well, that's great. I see your mom's car outside. I'll watch 'til you get in, O.K.?"

"O.K.," she said. "Goodnight Mr. Jordanger; goodnight Kenny."

I walked her to the glass door at the front of the shop and waited while Anna got into her mom's car. I waved and then watched them until they safely drove away.

I'd already done the closing paperwork so I could shut the store down for the night. Band practice started in an hour and the rest of the guys would be arriving soon. As usual, Kenny and I would run across the street to a little Italian place to grab a bite before practice started.

Over chicken parmesan and lasagna, Kenny and I discussed the dismal sales at the *Night Owl*. The business had been a raging success in 1998 and most of 1999. It was a place where novice music lovers and collectors alike came to buy hard to find CD's and rare vinyl. But at the end of 1999, Napster came on the scene and things changed drastically. My successful business saw declining sales and eventually it came close to floundering.

Only my hardcore customers who still wanted rare vinyl records stuck by me, but there weren't enough of them to keep my shop going. I'd had to take the job with *Wilson's Security Systems* to keep money coming in, and I was forced to cut the hours that the record store was open. Sometimes I met collectors there by appointment. Things got a little better when I put in a coffee bar. I was able to hire a kid and pay him a small salary to manage the shop during the day. Ironically, I sold more coffee at better margins than music. A culture developed around it as people seemed to enjoy sipping their mocha-lattes while they thumbed through music selections. However, sales at the *Night Owl* dipped again in 2006 when the economy tanked and people started losing their jobs. I was barely staying afloat as it was, but since I'd cut my debt to a bare bones minimum, I was able to stay open in the face of this new challenge.

When Kenny and I got back to the *Night Owl*, we saw that Monte had already arrived and let himself in. He was getting himself a free coffee and adding a shot of the scotch that I kept behind the register. He offered me some, but I declined.

"Look guys, we can't let this jam session go all night. I'm picking Melanie up at the airport at midnight."

I was surprised when they didn't complain. Despite the fact that they were both in their fifties, they acted like spoiled children whenever they thought Melanie was interfering with band practice. What they and the other band member, Joe, failed to realize is that we weren't that good. I personally knew that I was wasting my time with them. I had more experience than they did, and I could easily get other players who were better and possibly play some gigs. But they were dedicated, and I'd given up on being a serious musician a long time ago.

We played until 10:00 p.m. and then called it quits so I could leave to make the forty minute drive to the Atlanta airport. Melanie was flying back from Portland and her plane was scheduled to land at 11:00 p.m. She would have to de-plane the passengers, straighten up the cabin, and grab her suitcase so we planned to meet out front at midnight. When I stepped outside, the chilly October air stung my nostrils. It had taken until almost the end of October, but the Georgia summer heat was finally gone. Thanksgiving of 2007 was just around the corner and Christmas would follow soon after. That meant that Melanie and I would travel to another small town where I would be able to hunt and kill.

Chapter 8
Atlanta, Georgia, November, 2007

    Lauren crushed out her cigarette under her black, patent leather wedge boot and blew her last puff of smoke into the cold, gray November sky.
    "I told Denny he needs to take us out for Thanksgiving this year. Our group is too big for that pot-luck thing we did last year. We could close the office at noon and go to a nice restaurant. What do you think?"
    "I'm good for closing the office early on any day," I replied.
    "I know, right?" she said with a smile. "That corporate-Nazi, Sven, is on my last nerve. He just started and he already wants to know what we do for Thanksgiving and Christmas around here. I think he wants some kind of big "to do." He just doesn't understand that we're kind of laid back around here; thank, God."
    I smiled at Lauren's ability to succinctly summarize exactly what I thought about our co-workers. Sven was 6'3", good-looking, and extremely enthusiastic in a way that I found very annoying. He seemed to be under the impression that he'd been hired to bring big company corporate initiatives to our little of-

fice. He didn't seem to know that protocol dictated that he go through our corporate office instead.

"You and Melanie taking your annual "lonely flyers club" trips on Thanksgiving and Christmas this year?" Lauren asked.

"I suppose," I said casually but my pulse jumped a little.

"Don't you ever want to celebrate the traditional way? You're both welcome at my house, you know. It just seems so sad that you travel on every major holiday. You don't even go anywhere fun."

"Thanks for the offer, Lauren, really. But the truth is, I kind of like being "in between the lines" on those holidays if that makes any sense at all. I like not knowing where I will be and that I won't know anyone when I get there. I like seeing decorations that I had nothing to do with putting up and knowing that I won't have to take them down. I guess I just like the feeling that none of the traditions or craziness that goes along with the season has anything to do with me."

I looked away from Lauren and pressed my lips together hard. I wanted to reveal everything to her at that moment. I wanted to say "*I like it because, instead of hunting for that perfect gift, I like to hunt for that one, thrown away person.*" I wanted to say it, but I didn't dare.

Lauren's eyes narrowed. "You know, Mitch, I get that. Even a little too well, maybe."

I blinked hard with surprise. Had she heard what I was thinking? Or had I said the words out loud without realizing it, like the time I said the word *pink* to Ella? I searched her face to get a handle on what just happened, but she looked calm and thoughtful as usual. I had not revealed myself to her. I was still safe. Still safe, and still alone.

Lauren started working at *Wilson's* about eight months after I did. I instantly liked her quick wit and after a while we became friends. She made me chuckle once when she remarked that she thought of *Wilson's* as the place where former corporate greats went to die. Nearly everyone there was a former bigwig who had been down-sized or lost a business.

Fortunately, *Wilson's* was growing despite the economic downturn. Retailers and educational institutions wanted to protect themselves with surveillance equipment in the wake of 9-11, and the company had done a good job of positioning itself to provide those products.

Lauren and I left the smoking area and went back inside the brown, brick building that *Wilson's* occupied. It was only three stories high. Not a huge building, and yet the many vacant suites inside were a sad reminder of how badly the economy was doing.

"You would think that I'd at least take the stairs after having a cigarette," Lauren said as she pushed the button for the elevator.

"Do you want to?" I asked.

"No, not really," she replied, "I'm not in the mood."

A soft ding sounded and the elevator's double doors slid open.

We got on and began the short ride up to the third floor. Lauren was standing behind me.

"It seems like I'm not in the mood to do anything lately," she said. Her voice sounded very sad. "Nothing seems to go right for me anymore."

I couldn't see her face very well in the mirrored door, so I turned around to look at her. A single tear had begun to slide down her face.

"Honestly," she said as her voice cracked, "If it wasn't for Corinne, I don't think I could keep going."

I was fumbling for the right words to say, but failing miserably.

"Mitch, sometimes I'm ready to lay this burden down, you know?"

The Darkness Behind the Door

I remembered how Vodronika looked when I spotted her on Christmas Eve last year. Everything about her had said that she was ready to lay her burden down.

"It's O.K.," I said, "A lot of people feel that way. You just have to figure out who they are."

Lauren shot me a look as the elevator's soft ding sounded again. We had arrived at the third floor. The doors slid open and Lauren walked out of the elevator ahead of me. I looked at her back and wondered what she was thinking. She had confessed her suicidal tendencies, and I had responded by damn near confessing my homicidal ones.

That evening at the *Night Owl*, I obsessed about what I said to Lauren. I had to be more careful when I was around her. Lauren was not like Melanie. She did not live in a cocoon of her own making, and she had the ability to figure things out if her curiosity was aroused.

I closed up at the *Night Owl* and went home to spend another sleepless night lying next to Melanie while she snored. I tossed and turned as I alternately worried and then hoped that Lauren had discovered the truth. When dawn finally broke I got up, showered, and went into *Wilson's* early.

I was surprised when I saw that Lauren was already there. She had pulled boxes of Thanksgiving decorations out from the store room. She had been busy because most of the office was already decorated with cornucopias, cinnamon wreaths, and apple pie scented candles that we would never burn. When I found her, she was in the break-room trying to get a card-board turkey to stand up straight. Her back was to me, but I could tell by her soft sobs that she was crying. She wheeled around when she heard me walk in.

"Oh, Mitch! You startled me! What are you doing here this early?" she asked as she hastily wiped her tears from her cheeks.

"I woke up early and couldn't go back to sleep. You need any help?"

"No, no; thank you. I'm about done." She turned away from me again and continued to wipe her tears.

"Lauren, what is it? What's wrong? I can see that you're upset."

"I'm sorry," she said, "I came in early because I didn't think anyone would be here. I didn't want Corinne to see me cry."

She walked over to the small kitchen table and pulled out a chair and sat down. She put her elbows on the table and pressed her face into her hands.

"It's my ex-husband," she said, "He's making my kid crazy, I think. He barely sees her but when he does, he scares her to death with his temper. She's so depressed all the time that it just breaks my heart. I want to put her in therapy but..." At this point she burst into tears again.

"Don't let him see her," I said, convinced that I had solved her problem.

It's not that easy," she said between sobs. "We have joint custody. That means he can get her whenever he wants without my permission. I can't afford a lawyer to take him back to court to get full custody. Oh, he's such an idiot!" Lauren's sobs were being replaced with fury.

"Put her in therapy then," I offered.

I was beginning to feel like I couldn't help her with her problem. I had wanted her to let me in, but now that she had things weren't going the way I had hoped.

"I can't afford therapy, either. Look, Mitch, I'm sorry I've burdened you with this. I don't want to talk about it anymore."

She got up from the table and walked over to the counter where the coffee maker was. She took the decanter off the warming station and filled it with water. When she lifted the decanter to pour the water into the reservoir, her sleeve slid down her arm. I saw the distinct impression of a hand-print on her forearm. Someone had grabbed her so tightly that their hand had left a mark. I knew it had to be her ex-husband who had put the mark there. He must have put the bruise on her cheek as well.

At 10 a.m., Lauren went outside to smoke and I went with her. She smoked slowly and deliberately as if she were deep in thought. I watched every move she made so I could get another look at the bruise, but the coat she wore kept me from seeing it. I had learned my lesson about mentioning it, though. I wasn't going to press her about it after what happened last time. Instead, I decided to try and take her mind off it.

"I own three houses in St. Thomas," I told her.

She looked at me with surprise.

"And why are you here in Atlanta then?" she asked with her eyebrows slightly raised.

"I honestly don't know."

"Is it because of Melanie?"

"I guess so," I said. "She can retire from the airline soon with full benefits. I guess I'm waiting on that and it's hard to let go of the *Night Owl*."

"Forgive me for saying so, but it seems like your business plan where the *Night Owl* is concerned is outdated by about seven years. Wouldn't you agree?"

It hurt to hear someone say it out loud. To actually hear the words that the *Night Owl* would never come back. Not in its original form anyway.

"Your point is?" I asked sarcastically.

"My point is, Mitch, that your business plan is outdated *here,* in Atlanta. But in St. Thomas, they probably just got karaoke. My guess is that they don't have iPods and pc's like we do here, so they probably don't download music like we do. I bet they would shop at a record store there."

I sat quietly as I thought about her idea.

"Look," she continued, "research it on the web **today**, and then make some real plans to move to St. Thomas and live happily ever after, goof-ball. That's what I would do if I owned houses there. I would be gone before you could snap your fingers!"

"Really?" I asked. "You would pick up and leave everything, just like that?"

"Yes," she said seriously. "It would be a relief to put some distance between me and my ex. That would be reason enough, but to move somewhere like St. Thomas where it's so beautiful! It would be a dream come true!"

Through every meeting I attended that day, I thought about what Lauren had said. It would be great to move to St. Thomas and live in one of my houses, but I didn't know if it was safe for me to go back. Had enough time passed so that my former friends had forgotten about me? Or were they still there, waiting to see me pay for the murder I committed in the 1970s?

Chapter 9
Hilton Head Island, South Carolina, July, 1978

It seemed my poor Mia would have to suffer through her pregnancy during miserably hot summer days coupled with frequent power outages brought on by President Carter's failed economic policies. Long lines at gas stations and flared tempers were frequent occurrences, and I was glad that the houseboat floated on the cool water in Sea Pines Cove outside of town.

By her third month, Mia had chosen the name Mela for a girl or Milo for a boy. Each name was a mixture of her mother's name, Ella, and her own. She worried that I was disappointed because my name wasn't in the mix, so she was determined to make Martin Richard McCloud part of our baby's middle name. I didn't know how she would make Martin or Richard part of any girl's name, but I wasn't upset.

I was thrilled that we were expecting because the plan I came up with in New Orleans was finally coming true. For the first time since I killed the pedophile when I was fifteen years old, I was hopeful about the future. I had put my burning hatred of Mia's step-grandmother, Delphine Perry, aside and I was once again determined to change. I wanted to settle down and devote myself to taking care of Mia and the baby. I had already talked to Eric, Dave, and Vince about traveling less and following through with making the demo tape with the producer in Texas. Dave wanted to do it so he could be home more often with Jill and Eve, and Vince agreed just to keep the peace. Eric, however, still held back. Since I was a changed man, I kept my cool when he told me he didn't want to do it. I took pleasure at the shocked look on his face when he saw that I wasn't going to argue. I had finally found something to believe in because of Mia and our baby. It seemed that the devil inside me was disappearing.

"Marty!" Mia yelled as she stuck her head inside the kitchen's sliding glass door. "Shut that thing off for a minute!"

I hit the switch on the blender and the loud "whrr, whrr" sound it made grinded to a stop. I had been making a concoction of fresh fruit and honey mixed with ice.

"Marty, I can't take another one of those!" she laughed. "You make me drink three a day!"

"It's good for the baby," I told her. I poured the drink into a glass, sprinkled some granola on top, and set it before her. "You need to drink every bit of that."

"Right, and you get to drink every bit of **that**," she said. She smiled and pointed at the beer that was sitting on the counter next to the blender. "Life is so unfair."

I reached out and rubbed her growing belly. "Life is more than fair," I said. "Life is even kind sometimes. When will we feel it move?"

"The doctor said it will be any day now." She put her arms around me and I pulled her close. She pressed her face into my neck. After a minute, she took a step back to look at me.

"You're really happy about this, aren't you?" she asked. "You don't feel like we're going to hold you down? I know Eric is mad because you want to cut back on traveling….."

"Don't worry about Eric. He'll come around about the demo, you'll see. Everything is going to work out fine."

The phone rang from its place on the kitchen wall. Mia rolled her eyes with mock aggravation.

"I'm sure it's Mom," she said as she went to answer it. Ella had called almost every day since we found out that Mia was pregnant.

"Hi, Mom," I heard Mia say. I took my beer and went out on the deck to watch the water gently roll. I felt secure now that I had ensured my place in Mia's family. They were the only truly good people I had ever met. The pedophile had unleashed my darkness, but I was sure that Mia's family would show me the way back. After a few minutes, I heard Mia hang up the phone. She came outside and took a seat beside me. She had the frozen drink I had made for her in her hand.

"Mom wants to come for a visit next week. She wants to go shopping to get some things for the baby. You don't mind, do you?"

"Of course I don't mind. Ella is always welcome here."

Mia sat quietly and sipped her frozen drink. I could tell she had something she wanted to say.

"What's on your mind, Mia?" I asked. "I told you Ella is welcome here. And I'm not going to feel tied down after the baby comes."

"It's not that. It's the *Polargo*, Marty. It's too dangerous for a baby to live here. I know how much you love it, but if the baby ever fell into the bay…." She shuddered.

After my talk with Ella I knew how hard it was for Mia to live on the *Polargo*, let alone raise a child on it. I had figured that this talk was coming, but I hoped it wouldn't. I loved living on the *Polargo*. I was docked in a prime spot with a beautiful view and almost complete privacy. Coming home to the *Polargo* had kept me sane many times before. It had certainly saved Eric's life more than once.

"Well, what do you think?" Mia asked expectantly. She knew I didn't want to leave the *Polargo*. She had lived on the houseboat to please me, but like any good mother she wouldn't tolerate the danger for her child.

"I know how much it worries you," I conceded. "We'll find a place in town but I'll keep the *Polargo*, too. That way the baby can enjoy it out here when he or she gets old enough. Maybe we'll go fishing," I offered. I hoped by saying this that she would remember the happy times she spent fishing with her father, but a cloud came over her face instead. I could tell she was wrestling with the idea, but after a minute she nodded. She seemed to be letting it go for now, but I knew we would have this talk again.

The next day Mia and I took a road-trip to Savannah. Going there and stopping by *Jimmy's Bar* had become "our thing". When we arrived Mike escorted us to Sonny's booth, but Sonny wasn't there.

"Sonny will be out in a minute," Mike said briskly. "Melinda will be over to get your drink order."

His gaze lingered on Mia longer than I liked. I figured it was because he hadn't known that she was pregnant. He gave me a brisk nod and then disappeared toward the back of the bar where Sonny's office was located.

"Something must be up," I told Mia.

Melinda, a pleasant, middle-aged woman who had worked for Sonny for years, came over to the booth and took our order. She brought me a scotch on the rocks and got a coke for Mia. We waited for nearly forty-five minutes before Sonny finally appeared.

"Mia, you look radiant," he said as he kissed her hand. Then he leaned over the table and shook my hand. "Marty, it looks like fatherhood is agreeing with you already."

Before I could say anything there was a loud crash. Mike burst through the men's bathroom door carrying a limp man in a headlock. As Mike dragged him along, he knocked over one of the tables with the man's head.

"Sorry, Sonny!" Mike yelled without breaking his stride or losing his grip on the man.

"What's that all about?" I asked.

Sonny's eyes flickered with anger for the briefest moment, but they quickly became cool again. He was a powerful, guarded man who rarely let his mask slip.

"I apologize for all the unpleasantness," he said evenly. "That guy delivers liquor here and he always uses our bathroom. We caught him shooting up in there today."

I did my share of drugs, but I stayed away from needles and junk. I had seen too many friends lose everything trying to score the next hit. I suspected Eric of using because of the crowd he ran with, but he always denied it. Across the bar, Melinda and a bus boy were cleaning up the mess Mike had made. The customers who sat nearby had barely noticed the commotion. After a few minutes Mike appeared at Sonny's booth.

"He's never to come in here again," Sonny told him. The tone of his voice was quietly furious. "You call his boss. I don't want that scum delivering liquor to my bar."

"Right," Mike replied tightly. He looked at Mia again and then excused himself. I was really starting to wonder why he kept looking at her. I watched him walk away until my attention was diverted by Mountain, who had just walked in.

"Sonny, excuse me for a minute. I see someone I need to speak to."

I went over to where Mountain was shooting tequila at the end of the bar. His biceps were as big as ever and sun-burned from riding sleeveless on his Harley Davidson FSX Low Rider.

"Marty, how are you doing, man?" he asked when he saw me. He took a shot of tequila and grimaced as he put the glass down. "Want a shot?" he asked.

"No, thanks," I replied. "I've got my favorite drink right here. Listen, are you coming out to the *Polargo* for the shrimp festival next week?"

"Wouldn't miss it! Are you going to dock over at Harbor Town like you did last year?"

"Yep, all the boats will dock there in the harbor. We'll tie up together just like last year."

"I just hope you can get us back to Sea Pines Cove this year," he laughed. "Last year, you were so wasted you damned near took us out to sea!"

When the party ended last year I had gone two miles in the wrong direction. I was almost into open water before I realized what I was doing.

"Don't worry about it," I joked. "I have plenty of life jackets on board."

Mountain leaned towards me conspiratorially. I could smell the tequila on his breath. "Listen," he said. "I'm going over to this chick Rachel's house later on. How about coming with me? She's got a roommate."

"Thanks, but I'm here with Mia," I said. I jerked my thumb in the direction of Sonny's booth. "She's over there with Sonny."

"Aahh, the old ball and chain," he sighed. He looked like a deflated tire. "This isn't like you, buddy. She's stayed around way past her expiration date, don't you think?"

"She's pregnant," I replied.

Mountain's eyebrows rose. "Is this good news?" he asked.

"Yes, it is."

Mountain shot me a look.

"Really, it is," I told him.

Mountain had never seen my dark side, so he couldn't know that Mia and the baby were my salvation. He only knew me as the hard-partying lead guitarist for a locally popular band.

"Well, in that case, congratulations, man!" he shouted. "Now you have to do a shot with me!" He waved at the bartender. "Two shots of your best tequila for me and my buddy, Marty! He's about to be a dad!"

The bartender dipped the rims of two shot glasses into rock salt. He put two sliced limes on them and set them down on the bar in front of us. He took a bottle of Patron tequila from the case behind him and poured an extra-large shot into each one.

"On the house," he said as he gave me a nod. "Congratulations on becoming a father."

Mountain picked up the shot glasses and handed one to me.

"Here's to your kid, man!" he exclaimed.

We each threw the warm, kerosene tasting liquid into the back of our throats and then slammed our shot glasses down on the bar. Mountain took my hand and shook it vigorously.

"Congratulations again, man!" he said happily.

Everyone within earshot came over to shake my hand or slap me on the back. Mike was also sitting at the bar, but he didn't come over to congratulate me. He watched us with a cool, ambiguous expression. When I walked back to Sonny's booth, I felt like his eyes were burning a hole into the back of my head.

Later that evening, I sat on the *Polargo's* portside deck again and watched the tide come in. Mia had already gone to bed. It seemed like she was tired all the time lately, but her doctor said it would get better soon. I hoped she wouldn't try to use it as an excuse for not coming to the shrimp festival. I had let her beg out of it last year, but I wanted her to come with me this year. The festival was going to be a wild time, and I didn't trust myself without her there. Now that she was pregnant, I didn't want to lose her by doing something stupid like cheating on her. She hadn't been on a moving boat since the day she saw that little girl drown, but I wanted her to come with me anyway. She might not have the best time, but I knew I could keep her safe. I decided to manipulate her into going. I told her about the festival the next morning after breakfast. When I told her I wanted her to come, she looked at me like I'd asked her to swim the English Channel.

"Marty, I can't do it," she said, her voice trembling. Her face had gone pale.

"Come on, Mia. We'll take a slow ride over to Harbor Town and tie up with the other boats. You will be safe, I promise."

"Please don't make me," she pleaded. Her hands gripped her glass of orange juice so tightly that her knuckles turned white.

"Look, we'll be tied up with at least five other boats. Do you really think they would all sink at the same time? That's ridiculous!" I got up and walked into the kitchen to let her know that the conversation was over. She stayed on deck by herself for almost an hour before she tried to talk to me again.

"Marty, you don't understand," she said quietly when she finally came inside to find me. "Something happened to me when I was just a kid-"

"You're acting like a kid right now!" I exploded. "Can't you put it behind you? I've already invited everyone out here!"

"Please listen to me," she pleaded. You see, when I was-"

I put my hand up to silence her. I knew she was trying to tell me what I already knew. When she was just fifteen years old, she saw the Mississippi River suck a little girl down beneath its murky surface. Ella had told me about it, but she asked me not to tell Mia that I knew. I was keeping Ella's secret but it wasn't out of loyalty to her. It was for my own, selfish reason. I wanted to get my way with Mia.

"I agreed to leave the *Polargo* and buy you a place away from the water because of your ridiculous fears," I bellowed. "You know how much I love living on the *Polargo,* but I'm giving it up for you! All I ask in return is for you to come to this party with me. It will probably be the last one before we move. Honestly, I can't believe how selfish you are being right now."

With that, I stomped away. I was sure I would get my way because I knew how much Mia wanted to please me. Now that she was pregnant, she was more vulnerable than ever. She wanted me to love her and the baby more than anything. I heard her go into our bedroom and close the door behind her. I decided to leave her alone for a while to stew in it, so I untied one of my kayaks and paddled out into the bay. I was gone for at least three hours, but when I got back I saw that she was still in our bedroom with the door closed. It was time to change tactics. I had made her feel ashamed for being selfish, so now I would make her feel guilty by being kind. I opened the door and saw her lying on our bed. When I got closer I saw that she had been crying. I sat down beside her and gently rubbed her shoulders.

"Mia, listen, if you're too scared I'll call everybody and cancel. The shrimp festival is a tradition around here and I wanted to share it with you, but it's not that big a deal."

"No," she said sadly. "You already invited everyone and they're looking forward to it. If it's that important to you, I'll go, too."

I kissed each one of her eyelids and then gently made love to her.

On the night of the festival the guests started arriving at 5 p.m. I had told everyone we were shoving off at 6 p.m. sharp, whether they were on board or not. Festivities began in Harbor Town at 6:30 p.m., and I planned to be on time. Vince, Dave, and Jill were the first to arrive. Mountain and a girl I didn't know followed soon after, and Eric and his latest girlfriend, Dawn, brought up the rear. I mingled with everyone on the *Polargo's* starboard, portside, rear, and roof-top decks but Mia stayed in the kitchen with her hands tightly gripping the counter. It was almost time to pull up the anchor and go, so I went into the kitchen to prepare her.

"We're about to go," I said as I nuzzled the back of her head.

Her body was rigid against mine. I put my arms around her and kissed her shoulder. The girl who came with Mountain walked into the kitchen. She wore bell bottom jeans and a pink and yellow striped bikini top. I noticed that Mia pulled at her dress self-consciously to hide her belly. The girl walked over to one of the coolers and fished a beer out of the ice.

"I'm Lindsay," she said as she peeled the pop-top off the beer.

"Hi, I'm Marty," I replied.

"Actually, I know that," she said with a sly smile. "We've met before."

I didn't remember her but experience had taught me that when a girl said we'd met before, it meant that we had slept together. I realized that Lindsay and I had looked at each other a little longer than we should have.

"This is Mia," I said quickly.

Lindsay looked Mia up and down. "You're pregnant," she said flatly.

Just then Mountain burst in. He grabbed Lindsay up in a bear hug and spun her around. Lindsay's legs fanned out behind her and almost clipped Mia in the stomach. Mia pulled away from me and left the kitchen. Before I could follow her Mountain handed me a joint.

"Marty, my man!" he said as I took a drag. "Let's get this party underway before those crazy hippies you invited start jumping in the water. Eric dropped acid so he might jump at any second!"

Instead of checking on Mia, I went and started the *Polargo's* engine. Mountain pulled up the anchor and un-lassoed the rope that tied the *Polargo* to the dock. We slowly made our way out into Sea Pines Cove and then into the bay outside the cove. We arrived at Harbor Town in just thirty minutes. I dropped anchor a few yards out from where several yachts were docked in the marina. Before long, I saw Greg Harper's houseboat, the *Sainted Ava*, making its way over from Daufuskie Island.

"Hi, Marty!" he yelled when he got close enough to throw me a rope. As I tied our boats together, a beautiful girl without a bathing suit top waved at me from his starboard deck. The party began to get into full swing as the other boats began to arrive. The smell of boiled, sautéed, and fried shrimp permeated the air. On-board the *Polargo* a pot of low country boil, a mixture of shrimp, sausage, potatoes, and corn on the cob simmered on the stove.

Before long, some people from the other boats came aboard the *Polargo*. Mountain and Lindsay had some low country boil and then decided to go boat-hopping as well. I heard loud splashes as several people jumped into the Atlantic to have a swim. I had drunk my fourth beer so it was time for me to find the bathroom. Almost as soon as I was finished, someone knocked on the bathroom door. I opened it and saw that it was Dave's old lady, Jill. She took a deep inhale from a joint she was holding and then motioned for me to lean toward her. She blew the smoke she had inhaled into my mouth. When she finished, we both coughed.

Then she handed me the joint so I could take some drags of my own.

"You should check on Mia," she said while I puffed. Her voice had a wooden quality to it because she was so stoned. Her blue eyes were blood-shot from all the smoke.

I hadn't seen Mia in hours. "Where is she?" I asked.

"In your bedroom," she replied. I handed the joint back to her. She took it and held it away from her halter dress delicately, as though it were a cup of tea.

"I'll go check on her now," I told her. "See you later."

She nodded and went into the bathroom. When I got to our bedroom I tried to open the door, but it was locked. I knocked on it softly but there was no response.

"Mia," I called. "Mia it's me. Open the door."

After a moment I heard her get up off the bed and shuffle over to the door. The lock clicked and then she opened it just a sliver.

"Are you alright?" I asked but she had already walked away. She went back over to the bed and lay down. I walked over to the bed and sat down next to her. I gently brushed her hair back from her face.

"I don't feel good, Marty," she said. "You need to take me back."

"Don't be silly, babe. We just got here." My voice was soft and soothing, but I didn't plan on leaving the party anytime soon.

"My stomach hurts," she sobbed. "It's cramping." She drew her knees up toward her belly.

"Mia," I whispered, "we can't leave the party now. People are swimming out there. I could run somebody over if I tried to leave."

I rubbed her shoulders and smoothed her hair while she sobbed. After a while she fell asleep. I left her in our bedroom and went back on deck to rejoin the party. I found Dave, Jill, and Vince on the *Polargo's* rear deck. They told me that Eric had climbed up onto the roof and then jumped into the Atlantic. Mountain and Lindsay had not returned from boat-hopping. Everywhere I looked beautiful strangers and old friends ate, drank, smoked, or did whatever kind of drug they wanted. I sat down with Jill, Dave, and Vince for a while and looked out at the lights that dotted Harbor Town's marina.

At 8a.m. I awoke with a start. I sat up in my deckchair expecting to see Sea Pines Cove, but I saw murky ocean water all around me instead. The morning sea air was chilly and the sky was over-cast. A bell that was attached to a buoy made a lonely clanging sound as it went up and down in the mild ocean swells. When I tried to get to my feet, I felt extremely nauseous. I stumbled over to the *Polargo's* railing where I thought I would be sick. I wasn't able to vomit, so I gripped the railing tightly and waited until I felt better. When I opened my eyes and looked around, I saw that we were still tied up to the *Sainted Ava*. All the other boats had left, but the *Polargo* and the *Ava* were still tied together like two deserted orphans. It was deathly quiet except for the sound of the waves and the clanging bell. I had a bad feeling when I realized I hadn't seen Mia since last night. I hastily went into our bedroom to check on her. I breathed a sigh of relief when I saw that she was sleeping quietly. I wanted to lay down beside her, but I went to check if everyone who came with me was still aboard. Dave, Jill, and Vince were still sleeping in their deckchairs. I found Mountain and Lindsay in one of the bedrooms, but I couldn't find Eric or Dawn anywhere. I decided I didn't care where Eric was. For all I knew, he had drowned last night when he jumped off the *Polargo's* roof. As for Dawn, well, I didn't even know her. Those two weren't about to stop me from going home to nurse my hang-over. I pulled up the anchor and then untied the *Polargo* from the *Ava*. When I started the *Polargo's* engine, the sound cut through the quiet morning like a chainsaw. I carefully pulled away from the *Ava* and headed home to Sea Pines Cove.

The short trip home seemed to take forever. My head pounded and my stomach gurgled the whole way. Every swell the *Polargo* went over made me want to vomit. The engine sounded especially loud and its faint gasoline smell made me feel like I couldn't breathe.

I was so grateful when we reached Sea Pines Cove that I could have kissed the dock. With shaky hands, I steered the *Polargo* up to the dock, killed the engine, tied up, and then finally dropped anchor. I took a jittery walk to our bedroom and heaved myself onto the bed beside Mia. I fell deeply asleep. When I woke up again I saw that Mia was gone.

"Mia?" I called.

I sat up slowly because I was still fuzzy from all the booze and weed. I got to my feet and started toward the bathroom. As I walked over, I saw spots of blood on the carpet. They got bigger as I got closer to the bathroom. When I turned on the light, I saw Mia sitting on the floor next to the commode. The dress she was wearing had a huge stain of bright red blood on it and she was crying hysterically. I scooped her up in my arms and ran to the car. The hospital in Hilton Head was an hour away. I drove in a blind panic the whole way.

Chapter 10
Hilton Head Island, South Carolina, July, 1978

Vince had called ahead to let the hospital know we were coming, so there was a nurse waiting with a wheelchair when I pulled up. She whisked Mia inside and I pulled off to find a parking spot. Not until I sat inside the car with the engine off did I realize how big the blood stain on the seat beside me was. The essence of my child was spread across the tan, leather seat where Mia had sat.

My heart started to pound again as the reality of what I had done set in. I had pushed Mia into going out on open water and the stress had been too much. If our baby died Mia might never forgive me, and if Mia died her family would never forgive me either.

When I walked inside the emergency room, the atmosphere was humming with activity. People sat in the waiting area while others were rushed into the interior of the hospital. Mia wasn't anywhere to be seen, but the nurse who had wheeled her away was behind a counter in the center of the waiting room. She wore a white nurse's dress uniform with a navy cardigan that was tucked inside her collar so that it hung around her shoulders. I headed straight for her and interrupted her as she spoke to a lady who appeared to be suffering from heat stroke.

"Where's Mia Bouchard?" I interrupted; uncaring of my rude behavior.

"Martin McCloud?" she responded.

"Yes, where is she?"

The nurse turned to the woman I'd cut off who now glared at me. "Excuse me for one moment, please," she said as she walked from behind the counter to take my arm.

"Mr. McCloud, Mia has lost a lot of blood. She has been taken into surgery for a DNC and a blood transfusion."

"The baby....?"

"I'm very sorry, Mr. McCloud, but the baby didn't make it." She spoke in a hushed tone as she led me away from her station and the small crowd of people who gathered there. "She's in surgery now, but you can see her in her room when she gets out. It's number 383."

The back of my eyes stung and I couldn't hear well. The nurse's voice sounded as though it was coming through a wall, or as if either she or I were underwater.

"When will she be in her room?" I asked. There was a heavy pounding in my ears. Mia was going to hate me when she woke up and found out that the baby was dead.

The nurse blinked at me. "In about three hours. Mr. McCloud, are you O.K? Maybe you should sit down."

"I'll be back," I said. I had already started to walk away.

Back in the Challenger, I took a good look at the blood stain on the passenger seat. It had started to dry and turn into a dark, purplish color. It covered the seat entirely. It would make things even worse for me if I let Mia see it. I left the hospital and drove to a car wash to see if they could clean it. When the manager took a look at it, his mouth fell open with disbelief. It was obvious that he couldn't help me. Before he could ask me what had caused the stain, I jumped back into the Challenger and drove to a spot where I knew they sold used cars. When I pulled into the small, seedy looking dealership a guy came out of a trailer and waved before I'd even stopped the car. He waited like a dog expecting a bone while I turned off the Challenger's engine.

"How are you today, sir?" he asked. He spoke with a heavy southern accent and sweat dripped down his face. He took out a handkerchief from his back pocket and mopped his brow. "My name is Ed Hummel. What can I do for you?"

"I want to trade this car for any car you have on the lot."

Ed looked me up and down; then eyed the car. He took his time walking around it and even kicked the tires.

"You the owner?" Ed asked. His good old boy friendliness had turned into suspicion.

"That's right, Ed," I said, "I've got the registration in the glove compartment."

"O.K., then, Mr.-?"

"McCloud."

"O.K., Mr. McCloud, but I can tell you without even lookin' at the mileage on this car that you're gettin' soaked here. There's nothin' on this lot that can even touch this car. Why you want to do this anyway?"

"I have my reasons, Ed."

We walked through the lot and I found out that Ed was right; there wasn't much to trade for. I finally settled on a Dodge Monaco station wagon. It had seventy-five thousand miles and came complete with tacky wood paneling on the doors. My Challenger barely had fifty thousand miles and was in prime condition, but I didn't care if I left on a bicycle so long as Mia never saw that blood stain. Ed didn't care about the stain because of the great deal he was getting. I completed my transaction with him and went back to the hospital where I installed myself in Mia's room to wait for her to come out of surgery.

After two hours, a nurse wheeled Mia into the room. I watched her sleep and wondered what she was going to say to me when she woke up. Her doctor came in a little while later and confirmed that the baby had died, but he said Mia would be all right. She had lost a lot of blood but he had given her a blood transfusion. He said he wanted her to stay in the hospital for a few days to rest, but when Mia woke up she insisted that I take her home. She waited in a wheelchair on the curb while I went to get the Monaco. When I pulled up in it, she didn't ask what happened to the Challenger. In fact, she didn't seem to notice anything. She sat like a zombie and stared out of the window for the entire drive back to Sea Pines Cove.

The light in my beautiful Mia's eyes had gone out. I grieved for the loss of the baby, but she wasn't the same person anymore. She refused to talk to Ella when she called and she wouldn't see any of our friends. She even quit coming to the band's gigs. She stayed aboard the *Polargo* day after day and stared down into the brackish water. I was desperate to make her happy again because I could see that I was losing her. The plan I made in New Orleans was slipping away. I wanted to try for another baby, but every time I mentioned it she got a sad look in her eyes and turned away.

As we grew apart I got restless. I allowed Eric to shelve the plans for the demo tape again, and told him to book us into one of our regular gigs in Savannah. I hoped Mia would go because Savannah used to be special for us, but when I told her about it she barely looked at me. My heart was in the dirt, but I was glad when I loaded my guitar into the back of Vince's van. I wanted to get away from her for a while.

We played two sets at a club on the Savannah boardwalk that night and as usual, groupies waited for us until the last set was over. When Vince invited me to go to an after-hours party I didn't refuse. I also didn't refuse when one of the nameless girls who accompanied us put her hand in my pants. When we got to the house where the party was taking place, she and I didn't go inside with everyone else. We went to the beach and satisfied each other again and again until we passed out on the sand, half-dressed and exhausted.

I didn't know how long I'd slept, but the light in the sky was turning a pale shade of blue which indicated that the sun would be coming up soon. The tide gently came in. Waves rushed over themselves softly and sea gulls ran up the beach to avoid getting wet. The girl was still asleep beside me. I looked down at my pants and saw that they were unzipped and pulled down to my thighs. My shirt was ripped and buttons were missing. I hastily dressed myself and headed toward the house without waking my beach companion.

I opened the front door of the beach house to the sight of dozens of people laid out across the floor. They lay end to end and side by side. It was difficult to step over them without disturbing them. As I moved through the crowd in search of Vince, Eric, or Dave, I occasionally stepped on someone's hair or hand. I finally made it to the stairway where a sign that said "Serendipity" hung on the wall. I headed upstairs hoping to find Vince so I could get the keys to his van. I had to get home before Mia woke up. I was scared that if she realized I hadn't come home last night, it would be the last straw and she would leave me. Fortunately, I finally found Vince in one of the bedrooms. He was out cold. One of the girls who came with us from the gig lay beside him.

"Vince, I'm taking your keys, man." I whispered vehemently.

Vince only rolled over so I pushed his shoulder. "Vince, I'm taking your van. I've got to get home before Mia wakes up."

Vince looked at me without seeing me. "But I'm driving, man. I'm driving….."

I realized it was hopeless, so I looked for some paper and a pen in the drawer of the nightstand next to the bed. I scribbled *I took your car……Marty,* and placed the note on the nightstand. Then I walked out of the bedroom, down the stairs, and out the front door. Vince's '71 Volkswagen Van was parked close to the road so it wasn't hemmed in by the other cars. I climbed in and drove like a bat out of hell toward Hilton Head.

It was nearly 8 a.m. before I reached the houseboat. I hadn't known where I was going when I first left the beach house and I'd made some wrong turns. I nervously pulled off the two-lane road that ran by the *Polargo's* dock and hurriedly parked Vince's van next to the Monaco and my bike. If Mia was awake then she would know I had not come home last night. Maybe she would be furious and we would have it out. Maybe I had finally pushed her buttons enough to make her come out of her damned haze.

I walked briskly across the dock and stepped on board. I saw no sign of Mia in the kitchen, so I went into our bedroom. I expected to find her sleeping in there, but when I opened the door I saw that she wasn't there. I went out onto the portside deck, but I didn't see her there or on the rear deck either. I went through the kitchen to the starboard deck, but I still did not find her. I was beginning to think that she was so pissed when she woke up and found me gone that she had left the boat. I didn't expect to find her on the roof because she had always been too afraid to go up there, but as a last resort I went to the ladder and climbed up anyway. Upon reaching the top I found the story to be the same; no Mia. I went back down the ladder to the main floor. I felt shaky and unsettled. A feeling of dread made my bowels loose. Without knowing why, I went back to the starboard deck where Mia had cowered against the wall on the first night we met.

She'd been in the water so long that her body had drifted toward the boat where it was trapped like a piece of driftwood. She was floating face down. When I saw her I jumped into the water. I turned her over and saw that she'd been dead for hours. She had probably fallen or jumped shortly after I left for Savannah. I pulled her on board and held her tightly as I rocked back and forth. It wasn't until Vince showed up to reclaim his van that afternoon that she was taken from me and the police were called. They quickly determined that she had been in the water all night, and that I was in Savannah when her death occurred.

Chapter 11
Hilton Head Island, South Carolina, August, 1978

I didn't go to Mia's funeral because I couldn't face Ezra, Cara, or most of all, Ella. The service was held in New Orleans and she was laid to rest in the family cemetery at her grandparents' mansion. I disliked this because they hadn't loved Mia, and I would need their permission if I ever worked up the courage to visit her grave. Ella had told me that Delphine would inherit the property if she out-lived Mr. Perry. If that happened, it was not only possible but likely that Delphine would cut all of us off from Mia's grave forever. I obsessed about it day after day as I stumbled around the *Polargo* in a haze of grief fueled by booze and pills. I had quit answering my phone or checking my mail and I slept at odd hours. Many of my friends had given up on me, but Jill still came by with food and Vince sometimes tried to keep me company. Their efforts were wasted, though, because for me life had ended. Mia had killed herself because of me and there was nothing I could do about it. I hated myself and I hated the *Polargo* even more. I wanted to sink the damned thing and send it to a watery grave, but I couldn't let go of the exquisite pain I endured by living there. Everything about the *Polargo* reminded me of Mia. Sometimes when I first woke up, I believed she was still alive and on board somewhere. Then I would remember she was dead and relive the awful moment when I found her. I would go through losing her all over again. As painful as this was, I still wanted those precious moments when I believed she was alive. With every passing day, it seemed that I was losing my mind.

One evening when I stumbled into the kitchen to grab another beer, I noticed a pile of mail that was sitting on the counter. Vince had evidently brought it in from the over-stuffed mailbox outside when he came by earlier that day. A certain letter with familiar handwriting caught my eye. I picked the letter up and read the return address. It had come from Conti Street in New Orleans. It was from Ella. My hand shook as I opened it and began to read.

Dearest Martin

I think I understand why you didn't come to Mia's funeral, but please don't blame yourself for what happened. She was a fragile person and the loss of the baby was simply too much for her to bear.

You made Mia the happiest that I had ever seen her, and I know she loved you a great deal. Take comfort in knowing that she is with her father and your baby now. She would want you to go on with your life and be happy.

Love,

Ella

My fist closed around the letter and I raised it to my face, crushing it between my fingers. Ella thought I shouldn't blame myself, but if she only knew the truth. How differently this letter would read if she knew that Mia lost the baby and killed herself because I made her go out on the water. Ella told me Mia was fragile and asked me to protect her many times, but I ignored her requests to get what I wanted. I used Mia's kind nature against her because I knew she wanted to please me. Then I enjoyed myself at the party while she suffered in our bedroom alone, scared, and in pain.

I went into the bedroom and got some Xanax out from the nightstand. I didn't know or care how many pills I had already taken that day. I swallowed two of them dry as I looked at the photo Ella had given me of Mia when she was a little girl just coming back from a fishing trip. Our baby probably would have looked like her. Suddenly, I felt very sleepy. I felt the picture slip from my hand and heard it fall softly to the floor. I closed my eyes and lay back on the bed. When I awoke it was pitch black inside the bedroom.

"Mia?" I called but there was no answer.

Through the silence I heard the familiar thud of waves hitting against the *Polargo's* hull. The sound brought it all back. I remembered seeing Mia's body trapped against the *Polargo* as waves grotesquely pushed her lifeless body into the side of it. If only there was some way I could make up for what I had done. I wanted to make things right with Ella even though she didn't know I had betrayed her. I remembered again what Ella told me about her father's mansion where Mia was buried. Delphine would inherit it if Mr. Perry died first, but if Delphine died first, then Ella and her children would inherit. I knew what I could do to try to atone for taking Mia away from her family. I would kill Delphine. It would ensure that Ella never had to worry about losing her families' home or being cut off from Mia's grave. I had killed once to avenge myself and protect children from a pedophile. Now I would kill again to avenge Mia and protect the people I loved from losing their birth right.

The Darkness Behind the Door

I left for New Orleans at 3p.m. the next day. At midnight, I was parked down the street from Ella's home on Conti Street. Most of the house was hidden by the wrought iron fence, but the small corner I could see made my heart ache. I wanted to ring the bell so I could see Ella, Ezra, and Cara again but instead I took one long, last look and started for the Perry's mansion outside of town.

The sight of the mansion the second time around was no less impressive than it was the first time. I drove by it slowly so I could once again take in the massive Doric columns, the graceful verandas, the over-sized double-hung windows, and the winding driveway all framed by ancient oak and magnolia trees. I drove a mile down the road and parked the Monaco in a secluded spot near the levee. I got out of the Monaco and checked my watch; it was 2 a.m. I had made good time from New Orleans, but I would need to keep moving if I was going to kill Delphine before the sun came up. I started a light jog back toward the house until I recognized a fence that marked the beginning of their property line. The house was still several yards away but I wanted to get off the main road now that I was closer. I decided to make the rest of the trip through the trees that bordered the house on all sides. I stepped over the fence and carefully made my way into the forest. The thick branches blocked out the moonlight and made it hard for me to see where I was going. I felt, rather than saw, my way through. When I finally emerged my skin was stinging with tiny cuts and scrapes, but I pressed on. I couldn't see the house yet, but I hoped I was going the right way. I passed an old corn crib and a small shack, and then I spotted an eerie sight in the moonlight up ahead. In the distance, four tombstones peaked out above a black, wrought iron fence. When I got closer, I realized that one of the headstones looked newer than the others. I couldn't read the name in the dark, but I knew instantly that it was Mia's grave. I stared into the lifeless eyes of the marble angel statue above her grave until I felt a tremendous pounding inside my ears. Blackness, darker than the night, overtook me and I fell forward. My head hit against the wrought iron fence as I crashed down to the earth. When I came to, I sat up carefully and gingerly rubbed the place on my head where I hit the fence. The skin felt fleshy and sticky with blood. I had no idea how much time I had lost while I was unconscious and it was too dark to see my watch. I got to my feet, more determined than ever to kill Delphine now that I had seen Mia's grave. I started walking again until the house finally came into view. No lights were on so I made my way around to the courtyard Delphine had refused to show to me, Cara, and Mia on the night she reluctantly gave us a tour. When I reached the double French doors that opened onto their sitting room, I took out a credit card and easily jimmied the out-dated lock. Apparently the Perry's weren't very worried about security, which was strange considering Delphine's psychopathic obsession with the expensive things the house contained. I moved through the dark sitting room as quickly as I dared. I didn't want to knock over any of the figurines that I knew were scattered around like landmines. When I made it through the room I walked into the grand hall. There was enough ambient light to allow me to see my watch. It was 3:15a.m. I wanted to get upstairs and find the master bedroom because I figured Delphine was sleeping there. At the stairwell, however, I hesitated. I knew from the last time I visited that the stairs were going to creak as I climbed them. If someone heard me and came out into the hall, I was cooked. As I stood at the bottom of the stairs trying to decide what to do, I heard a door open from somewhere in the house. I froze as Harold appeared like an apparition in the kitchen doorway but, thankfully, he didn't see me. Instead of coming toward me, he walked across the hall and opened a narrow door that I hadn't noticed before. He went inside the doorway and disappeared. Unsure of what to do, I stayed frozen at the bottom of the stairs for several minutes until I forced myself to get moving. I ran up the stairs quickly with them creaking under every step. When I reached the second floor, I flattened myself against the wall while I tried to catch my breath.

Delphine hadn't shown us where the master bedroom was so I was going to have to figure it out by a process of elimination. I knew the first door along the hall belonged to Mr. Perry's study. When I passed the open door I sucked my breath in sharply because Mr. Perry was sitting at his desk. A wave of relief washed over me when he let out a loud snore. He was asleep in his oversized, leather-bound chair. The crystal decanter that usually resided on his bookshelf was sitting on his desk in front of him. The crystal glass beside it was still half-full with liquor. Even though he was asleep, I found his presence unnerving. If he woke up, things would quickly get out of control. I moved past his door quietly and made my way over to the room that I suspected was the master bedroom. When I opened the door it made a long, slow creak. I quickly stepped inside and tried to look around in the dark. As my eyes adjusted, I could just make out the toile wallpaper and the shape of a large bed that unfortunately, was completely made up and empty. There was no sign of Delphine anywhere. I checked my watch again; it was 3:40 a.m. I was going to have to give up on my mission and get out of the house before the servants woke up. The Monaco needed to be moved before anyone saw it by the levee and got curious. I turned on my heel and went back downstairs. Frustrated, I walked back through the sitting room taking much less care about the noise this time. I was about to let myself out through the double French doors when I spotted Delphine asleep on the sofa. There were two empty martini glasses next to an overstuffed ashtray on the coffee table beside her. I had obviously walked by her when I came in, but she hadn't heard me. She was sleeping so hard she was even snoring. This was my chance. I walked over to her and placed my hands around her throat. Her eyes flew open and she grabbed at my arms. She tried to throw me off, but it was no use. I squeezed tightly until she went limp beneath my hands. The cold, intimidating woman who had controlled everyone around her was finally dead. Her dark eyes that had looked us over with such contempt on the night we visited were now dull and peaceful. I felt relieved that she was dead. I knew at once that I had done the right thing by killing her. She wasn't going to bully her staff or threaten Ella and her children anymore. I released her frail, lifeless body and went back over to the French doors to let myself out. I stepped outside and turned around to push the doors closed behind me. As I did, I looked through the glass in the door and saw that someone from inside the house was watching me. Harold was standing in the doorway of the sitting room and he was looking directly at me. I took off running and didn't stop until I reached my car.

As I sped back to Hilton Head I thought about all of the mistakes I had made, such as leaving fingerprints everywhere along with drops of my own blood. Worst of all, Harold had seen me. When I decided to kill Delphine, I did it impulsively through a haze of grief, booze, and pills. I hadn't done any planning because I didn't care if I got caught. Now that Delphine was dead and Harold saw me kill her, I suddenly cared very much. I wondered what was going on back at the Perry's mansion. Harold was probably telling the police he had seen me while Mr. Perry phoned Ella to get my address. The Louisiana police would alert the police in Hilton Head. They would have a team waiting to arrest me when I pulled up to the *Polargo*. I desperately wanted to get back home, but every mile I covered felt like one step closer to my own funeral.

Relief washed over me when I got to the *Polargo* and saw that the police weren't there. However, I knew they could show up at any minute, so I had to keep moving. I had formulated a plan during the drive that, if successful, would ensure that I never had to worry about being arrested for Delphine's murder again. I had fantasized about sinking the *Polargo* before because I hated it, but now I was really going to do it. I was going to sink it and make everyone think I had committed suicide by drowning when it went down. Then I would leave Hilton Head forever and start over in a new place.

I stepped aboard the *Polargo* and immediately went out onto the rear deck where my two kayaks were tied up and floating. I quickly untied one of them and let it drift off into the cove. I then grabbed a life-jacket, rain slicker, baseball cap, compass, and my diving knife and flashlight. I took all of the gear and placed it near the one remaining kayak that was tied up to the houseboat. I hurriedly went inside to the bedroom Mia and I had shared and grabbed a bag from the closet. I packed a t-shirt, one pair of jeans, tennis shoes, and some underwear and socks into the bag. Then I got the titles to the Monaco and my motorcycle and put them inside the bag as well. The bag was still mostly empty and that's how I needed it because I planned to fill the rest of it with cash.

I got my pistol out from the nightstand and carried it outside to the rear deck. It was loaded, so I carefully laid it beside the kayak and the other equipment. If I had to use the gun it would be because of dire circumstances. Bull sharks, the only sharks that can survive in both fresh and salt water, were frequently spotted on Hilton Head because they liked to have their young in the brackish waters around the island. They were known to be aggressive and one could easily flip my sea kayak. My vision would be severely limited with only a flashlight to guide me, but if one attacked, I would do my damndest to shoot the bastard.

    There had been very little to do at the houseboat. It wasn't hard to disassemble the selfish life I had led because I wasn't taking anything with me. The *Polargo* was the last reminder of the night I killed our baby and lost Mia, so I would be glad when I was rid of it. With things in place at the *Polargo,* I grabbed the bag and got on my bike for the last ride I would ever take on it. After I went to the bank, I was going to see the one man who could help me find redemption by starting over.

Chapter 12
Hilton Head Island, South Carolina, August, 1978

Sonny Domicco took a slow puff from his cigar and then flicked the ashes into a black ashtray that sat on the desk before him. He looked down at his hands and then over at the bag of cash I had brought as he considered my plan and the part I had asked him to play in it. I would give him the free and clear titles to my bike and the piece of shit Monaco, plus $12,000.00 in cash if he would provide a new identity for me, a plane ticket to St. Thomas, and a ride to the Savannah airport. We were sitting inside his private office in the back of *Jimmy's Bar*. Mike, his ever present bodyguard, stood behind Sonny and watched me with a steely gaze.

"You know, Marty," Sonny said finally, "the police said you didn't have anything to do with that girl's death."

"That's right," I replied, pissed that he hadn't mentioned Mia by name. I also wondered how he knew that the police had cleared me as a suspect in her death.

"Is there something you'd like to tell me about it, then?" he asked. He looked at me like a father who already knew his son had broken the window, but he wanted a confession as well.

"No."

"You want to tell me why you're doing this then?"

"That's my business, Sonny."

I left *Jimmy's* knowing that Sonny and Mike both thought I wanted to disappear because I killed Mia. They were right to believe I was a murderer, but they were wrong about who it was that I had killed. But whatever they thought, it didn't matter because they weren't the kind of upstanding citizens who would go to the police. Sonny had agreed to provide the fake identification, the airline ticket to St. Thomas, and transportation to the Savannah airport as well.

In the summer time in South Carolina, the sun didn't set until 8 p.m. At 9.p.m, I untied the *Polargo* and started the engine. We moved slowly through the "no-wake" zone in Sea Pine's Cove and turned left at the last dock that marked the end of the cove and the beginning of the bay. It was smooth sailing as I made my way over to Harbor Town where I had tied up with the *Sainted Ava* on the fateful night of the shrimp festival.

I passed the yachts that were docked in the marina and then the last sight of land disappeared into the distance behind me. Waves began to rock the *Polargo* as we moved out into the sea but we were doing all right. Gradually, the waves got higher and the new moon provided no light.

I sailed into blackness using the *Polargo's* depth-finder as a guide. I wanted to sink it in two hundred feet of water or more. When the depth finder indicated I was in two hundred fifteen feet of water, I made a note of my location by looking at the navigational coordinates and killed the engine.

I went below deck and opened the *Polargo's* bailing holes. Now there was no time to spare. I moved quickly to the kayak where my diving flashlight was already firmly tied to the nose. It would act as a lantern on my long trip back to shore. The flashlight was made for underwater visibility for as far as ten feet, so I figured I would be able see well enough ahead of me out over the ocean's surface. However, everything to my right, left, and behind me would be completely black. I pulled my rain slicker and life jacket on and then pulled my baseball cap down low over my eyes. I put the compass, the pistol, and the diving knife inside a dry bag and hooked it to the kayak. I was ready to leave the sinking houseboat.

The *Polargo* was taking on water quickly. Its flat hull wasn't designed for rolling waves and ocean swells and it began listing at thirty degrees sooner than I expected. I stepped carefully onto the kayak and paddled as fast as I could to get away from the *Polargo*, so I wouldn't be pulled under by any suction. I'd heard that suction from sinking boats was really a myth, but out there alone in two hundred fifteen feet of water, I wasn't taking any chances. I paddled for some time without knowing how far away I'd gotten since I had no lights behind me. I dipped my paddle into the cold water alongside the kayak to steer the nose back around toward the *Polargo*. As I came around my flashlight lit the exposed hull in piecey spots through the darkness. The *Polargo* was capsizing on the starboard side, exactly where I wanted it to. Water rushed into the cabin and flooded the kitchen. I figured our bedroom was completely underwater by now. A chill went through me as I thought of everything I had shared with Mia being taken over by cold, deep ocean water.

The *Polargo* listed at ninety degrees for maybe five minutes before it succumbed completely. When it slipped under for the final time, it went quietly and there was no suction. The houseboat's design had made it heavy and unwieldy in the white-capped waves that rocked it and rushed inside. Somehow the *Polargo* had seemed ready to meet its fate. It had gone to its watery grave without a fight, just like Mia must have on the night she stepped off its side. I knew I needed to get moving if I didn't want to follow the *Polargo* down to the depths. I steadied the kayak with my paddle and then began my long trip toward the marshes where Sonny's *Shrimp House* restaurant was located. I was in pretty good shape but I knew the odds were against me. Kayaking the ocean for fifteen miles in the dark of night was a suicidal proposition, and if I had cared that much about living I would have been scared out of my mind. I only had the compass to guide me now. Were it to be snatched from me by a wave I could be lost and paddle around for hours in the wrong direction.

    I kayaked with the best form I could muster and rested when I needed to. As I got closer to shore the waves got rougher. The rain-slicker and the baseball cap I wore did little to keep the ocean spray from getting into my eyes. The effort wore long and I could barely keep paddling. If I could just make it to the marshes that flowed behind Sonny's restaurant; I would be home free. I would be back in calm lagoon waters.

    Finally, I reached the mouth of the marsh that I recognized as the one behind Sonny's restaurant. I had been a guide on many kayaking trips that left from behind his place before. The restaurant was an old house with a foundation that was built into the side of a hill. At the front of the house, the foundation sat evenly with the top of the hill. It stretched out on poles over land that fell away down toward the marsh. Underneath the house, kayaks and other boating equipment hung from hooks that were screwed into the beams from the flooring overhead.

    I turned off my diving flashlight as I neared the muddy shore. The restaurant had been closed for hours, but now that the *Polar-*

go was sunk and I was about to assume a new identity, I didn't want to take any chances on being seen.

Sonny would be waiting in the parking lot with my new identification, my plane ticket, and the bag I had packed and given to him earlier that day. I was dead tired, but I forced myself to keep paddling until the kayak ran aground. I stepped out of it with wobbly legs and then my left leg suddenly disappeared into mud up to my thigh. I felt the piercing stab of something scrape it all the way up. I struggled to free myself, but I only sank deeper. My urge to fight was strong, but I stayed still and stabilized. I gripped the kayak carefully with both hands and put my weight on my free leg. Slowly, I pulled my left leg up from the mud and got another scrape as I freed it. Water quickly ran into the hole and mud caved back in on itself. I managed to see what had scraped me before the treacherous hole was able to hide itself again. An oyster shell had sliced my leg from my knee to my thigh and blood dripped down to my ankle.

I pulled my cap, life jacket, and rain slicker off and was grateful to be free of their dampness. I left everything where it was except for the pistol. Even though I considered Sonny a friend, it had occurred to me that he could keep the $12,000.00 I'd given him plus the $100,000.00 he was holding for me if he made sure that the death I had staged became reality. As I looked up the hill toward the restaurant, a dark figure stepped out from the shadows. I put the pistol in the waistband of my shorts and climbed up the muddy hill. When I got closer, I saw that it was not Sonny but Mike who waited for me.

"I didn't think you'd make it," he said. He didn't sound thrilled that I had. He threw a towel at me and I began to dry my hair and the rest of my body. Last, I carefully mopped the blood that continued to drip down my leg.

"Come under the house," Mike said. He turned around and disappeared back into the shadows.

I put my right hand on the pistol and followed Mike. Underneath the house, he stood in the dark amid kayaks and canoes. Only the ghostly light from his lit cigarette made him visible.

"Your bag is over there." He gestured with the cigarette over to where rafts were piled from the floor to the ceiling.

I looked at him sideways as I made my way over to the rafts. It was hard not to trip in the dark over all the equipment while trying to keep an eye on Mike at the same time. I walked behind the rafts and saw that the bag I'd given Sonny was indeed sitting there. I was hidden from Mike, so I carefully removed the pistol from my waistband and checked the contents of my bag. Good old Sonny; my clothes and a package that looked like the money he'd been holding for me were all inside. Feeling a bit more relaxed, I quickly took off my wet clothes and put on the jeans, t-shirt, and tennis shoes that I'd packed earlier that day. I stepped out from behind the rafts. Mike had his back to me but he turned around when he heard me walk toward him.

"Your flight is at 2 a.m.," he said. "It's just after midnight now so we better get going." He turned and walked up the hill toward the parking lot.

A maroon Cadillac sat in front of the restaurant in an otherwise deserted parking lot. I thought Sonny would be inside, but he wasn't. Mike took the wheel and I climbed into the back seat. It seemed like they had come through for me, but I still felt more secure sitting behind Mike. Despite my paranoia, I fell asleep before the car even made it to the highway.

Out at sea again, I was aboard the Polargo as it sank into the black ocean. To my relief, a submarine surfaced. People peered at me from the bridge. They wore heavy coats and boxy hats. One of them threw me a line which I tied around my waist, and then I swam off the sinking Polargo to-

ward the sub. When I got on board I was surprised that no one spoke English and despite their heavy clothes, it wasn't cold. The sub moved stealthily through the ocean toward a cove that looked like a regular street. We turned into the cove, and I saw that the ocean water flowed at a level that was exactly even with the manicured lawns of the houses we passed. In each driveway sat a person in a single lawn chair in a relaxed pose, and beside each person was a dog that stood alertly. The further down the street of water we moved, the more intently I looked at the relaxing individuals in their lawn chairs. I came to realize that each person was really dead, and their dogs were standing guard beside them. I carefully studied one person as we passed, and the dog beside him began to bark at me…

I awoke with a start to the sound of a barking dog. Mike had pulled up in front of the door to Delta check-in at the Savannah airport. It was 1:30 a.m. I had slept during the entire drive from Sonny's restaurant to the airport. The place was completely quiet and nearly deserted except for the sound of planes taking off and landing and the barking dog.

"You have thirty minutes," Mike said in a clipped tone.

I climbed out of the Cadillac still not fully awake. Mike lit another cigarette and stared straight ahead.

"Mia was a nice girl," he said as I slammed the back passenger door shut.

"Yes, she was," I replied.

Mike got out of the Cadillac and walked around the front of it until he came and stood directly in front of me.

"I never liked you, you know. Every time you came into *Jimmy's* I liked you even less. I always knew there was something about you that wasn't right. It's just a shame that Mia had to pay for it."

I wanted to plant my fist into his jaw, but I had a plane to catch. We stood and stared at each other, two killers daring the other one to make the first move.

"Sonny says you are never to show your face in South Carolina again," he continued, "but as for me, I hope you do because I will gladly kill you myself."

I wanted to make him eat his words, but I was so close to starting my new life. I didn't want to call attention to myself by getting into a fight with Mike outside the airport. I clinched my fists at my sides and nodded in agreement. He turned on his heel and angrily walked back around to the driver's side of the Cadillac and got in. He jerked the gear into drive and gunned the Cadillac forward.

I wheeled around to the sliding glass doors of the airport fully awake now because of my confrontation with Mike. Every muscle hurt and I was starving, but there would be no time to eat before I boarded the plane. The airport was nearly empty so I easily made my way over to the check-in counter. The ticket agent was busy with the only other person in line, so I pulled my ticket out to read my new name. The ticket read *Mitchell Jordanger*. The agent finished with the guy in front of me, so I moved forward and handed him my ticket. His eyebrows rose as he looked it over and then looked back at me. My heart skipped a beat as I waited for him to say that he knew I was really Martin McCloud, and not Mitchell Jordanger.

"I.D.?" he said at last.

I jumped slightly. "Oh, of course," I said.

My pulse raced as I realized I hadn't checked my bag for my new passport. I had been so anxious about the money that I had neglected to look for it. I felt around inside my bag for what seemed like an eternity. Finally, my fingers closed around a thin, rectangular object that had been tucked into a side pocket. I pulled it out hastily. The agent was staring at me so I handed it to him without looking at it first. I held my breath as he looked at the passport and then at the ticket. He scribbled something on my ticket and then looked at me again.

"Are you checking any bags?" he asked blandly.

"No, I'm not," I told him.

He casually handed my passport and boarding pass over and then pointed to his right.

"Your gate is down that way," he said. "Have a nice flight."

The sleepy guard on duty at the security gate didn't even go through my bag. It was a relief because I didn't want him to get curious about the $100,000.00 that was inside. At last I made it to my gate where a beautiful black stewardess waited to take my boarding pass. She was tall and slim with even features and high cheek bones. Her long ringlets were pulled back into a pony-tail and she wore a colorful scarf that seemed to promise carefree island days. She smiled at me as she took my boarding pass

"Welcome aboard, Mr. Jordanger," she said. The name came out "Jorr-dan-gerr" when she spoke in her lilting British-Virgin Island accent. I had read my new name on my ticket only minutes before, but hearing someone address me by it was still a bit of a shock. I stared at her mutely. She returned my stare with a look of confusion and glanced at the boarding pass to see if she had made a mistake. My mind finally snapped to attention.

"Yes, thank you," I replied. "Uh, thank you very much."

I boarded the plane and found my seat as I heard her greet the only other passengers on the flight, a teen-aged couple who appeared to be headed for a vacation. I threw my new passport onto my seat so I could look it over when I sat down. I stowed my bag in the over-head compartment and settled into my seat. I opened up the passport and saw my photograph above my new name, *Mitchell Jordanger*. I would never know how Sonny had pulled it off, but the passport looked authentic in every way. As the plane took off for the two hour flight to St. Thomas, I quickly fell asleep once more.

Chapter 13
St. Thomas, U.S. Virgin Islands, March, 1979

"Mitch! Mitch!!! The tourists are here!"

I heard Marquita's throaty, cheerful, island-accented voice calling me. I was working in back of the grass-roofed, beach-side hut I called *Jimmy's* in honor of Sonny's place back home

It had been seven months since I'd arrived in St. Thomas and I had been a busy man. I gave snorkeling, kayaking, and diving tours to tourists from behind *Jimmy's,* and I owned three houses and a real estate brokerage as well. It had been easy to get the bar and tours added to the tourist circuit. A few bribes to some powerful locals, and I was in business.

"Leon will take care of them," I called back to Marquita.

She appeared in person alongside the hut, hands perched on jutting hips.

"Mitch, don't you know Leon isn't here? Someone needs to get these people a drink before they take off with you."

I should have fired Leon a long time ago, but I didn't because I liked him. I kept him on even though he treated his job like an after-thought and drank more liquor than the customers did. Eric, Vince, and Dave used to work harder after pulling an all-nighter than Leon did on his best day.

"All right," I said, "I'll take care of them."

I had already pulled out six two-seater ocean kayaks from the small shed behind the bar and placed them on the beach in rows. Since I had Leon's job to do as well, I made quick work of getting the paddles, life-jackets, and snorkeling gear out. I laid them beside each kayak and walked the short distance over hot sand to *Jimmy's Bar*. Twelve tourists mingled inside.

"Hi, there," I said cheerfully, ready to do my bit as the cool, island bartender and tour guide. "What can I get for you before we start the tour?"

"You Jimmy?" asked a short, chubby woman with long, red hair and pale skin. She spoke with an Australian accent.

"No, I'm Mitch," I said as I walked behind the bar. I didn't tell her I was the owner of *Jimmy's*. I had figured out a long time ago that tips were better if the tourists thought I worked for someone else.

My humble establishment offered beer, sodas, and rum punch that was pre-mixed. It made things simple for Leon so he could keep up. He sometimes had trouble because he drank two drinks for every one that he poured. There was still no sign of him anywhere, so I quickly served each of the tourists a drink. When they were finished, I led them down to the beach. I let them choose their kayaks and then I walked in front of the group and stood near breaking waves. It was time to give them the same friendly speech I gave to every tour group. It included a brief demonstration on paddling and then I pointed out the cliffs we were going to kayak to. I briefed them on the signals I would give to tell them whether to paddle or stop. Then I went to each person and checked that they were wearing their life jackets correctly. After I checked them all, I went in front of the group again and instructed them on how we would enter the water. I would go first in my single kayak and wait for them off-shore. They would work in teams of two and enter the water one kayak at a time. When they got past the breaking waves they would paddle around near me until the last boat joined us. Once we were all in the water, they were to follow me in a straight line with a kayak length between each boat. This was to prevent the less skilled ones from crashing their kayaks into each other. With all the instructions given, I carried my kayak into the surf and nimbly climbed on. I paddled through white-capped waves out into deeper, calm water and waited for the next boat to join me. If Leon had been there he would have helped them climb into their boats. Fortunately, everyone made it in and past the waves without incident.

Once I made sure everyone was accounted for, I paddled to the front of the line and led them toward the steep ocean-side cliffs where we were going to snorkel. As we made our way over, I looked back at the group to see who was struggling. One couple was starting to lag behind so I stopped the progression and paddled back to them.

"How's it going?" I asked as I came alongside their boat.

"It's not," the woman replied, annoyed. She was petite but muscular. "We keep knocking our paddles together because he wants to do it all himself."

"Yes," I said, trying to keep things light. "We have a saying around here that two-seater kayaking should be required in premarital counseling. It can test even the best relationship. Tell you what might help." I pointed at the guy, "You tell her when to paddle and count it down." I looked back at her. "You paddle on his count. That way you won't crash your paddles together and you'll make some headway."

They gave it a try and the boat moved forward successfully. I left them and paddled back to reclaim my place at the front of the line. As I did I noticed that a few of the kayaks had drifted, but no one appeared to be in any danger. When I made it to a spot about eight yards from the cliffs, I waited until everyone caught up and motioned for them to circle their boats around mine.

"We'll tie our boats together here," I told them.

I dropped a small twenty-five pound anchor into the clear ocean water. I took out a rope from my dry-bag and tied one end of it to the hook on the nose of my kayak. The rest of the rope was coiled in a big loop. I held it up over my head for everyone to see.

"I'll pass this to the person next to me," I said as I handed the rope to the Australian woman who was in the kayak on my right. "Make a loop around the metal piece you see there at the nose of your kayak, and then pass it to the person in the next boat. Once we're all tied together, we're going to get into the water and swim over to those cliffs. We're going to swim in a straight line, again leaving about one swimmer's body length between you. When we get to the lagoon on the other side of the cliffs, you can swim around at your leisure and check things out. But first, let me show you how to enter the water, so you don't flip your kayak over on top of you. Then I'll show you how to get back onto your boat in water that's too deep for you to stand."

While they bobbed alongside each other and passed the rope around, I carefully slid backward and pulled my legs out of my kayak's interior cavity. I dangled one leg over the side and carefully brought the other leg around to meet it. Now I was sitting sideways on top of my kayak. I leaned backward slightly so my weight was evenly distributed. Then I rolled over onto my stomach and slid off the side.

"Try to keep the kayak from flipping over by keeping your weight distributed evenly," I told them as I treaded water beside my kayak.

I reversed the process by grabbing onto the boat with both hands and then pulling my torso onto it. I threw one leg over the kayak while I held it steady in a bear hug. I inched my way around so that I was lying lengthwise on the kayak. I sat up with my legs dangling over each side. Then I pulled them inside and slid into my seat once more."

"You make it look easy," the red-headed Australian woman said skeptically. Her pale skin was beginning to burn in the sun.

"Don't worry," I said, "You won't sink the boat if you do happen to flip it over, and I'll be here to help. After you've had time to explore, I'll blow my whistle three times to signal that it's time to swim back to the kayaks."

The man in the blue kayak on my left strung the rope through the hook on his kayak and then handed it to me. I completed the circle by tying the rope to my hook.

"Now, everyone in the water and let's start swimming," I told them.

Some people jumped in right away, but others were more wary. Eventually they all got in. I was glad no one had asked me about sharks. We were swimming in forty feet of water and their appearance was a possibility. I had seen one or two on the tours before but they never ventured very close. Fortunately, the group enjoyed snorkeling without incident. I was able to show them eels, angel-fish, and some large grouper. At one point, a sea turtle swam through and gave everyone a thrill. After an hour, I sounded the three whistles and we headed back to the boats.

Back on shore, I thanked everyone and recommended a few places they could go to for dinner. This last gimmick was a way to steer them to places my friends owned or operated. Leon still hadn't shown up, so I stowed the equipment inside the shed and went inside *Jimmy's* to tend bar. I got my personal stash of high-end scotch out from its hiding place behind the register and poured myself a tall shot. After a few more, I was beginning to feel sleepy. No one had come into the bar for an hour, so I went outside to where I had hung a hammock up between two palm trees. I laid down in it and swayed gently in the steady breeze coming off the ocean. Judging from the sun's position in the sky it appeared to be around 3 p.m. I settled back to watch the stirring palm leaves against a back drop of bright, blue sky. When I opened my eyes again the palm leaves were still stirring, but the sky was dark blue. The sun had slipped so far down that only half of it was still visible above the horizon. I hastily got to my feet and went inside *Jimmy's* where I found Leon tending bar for two men who looked like they were in their early twenties.

"Here he is," Leon said as he took a sip from a cup he had behind the bar. "Mitch, these two want a sunset dive."

"That's right," one of them said. "I'm Steve and this is Will."

I reached out and shook each man's hand. I recognized Steve's accent immediately. It was southern, but it had a hard edge to it. A pang of sadness shot through me because he sounded like Ella.

"Where you guys from?" I asked.

"I'm from New Orleans, Louisiana and my friend here is from Baton Rouge. You sound like you're from somewhere in the south, too. Tennessee, maybe? Am I right?" Steve asked good-naturedly.

"Uh, no," I replied hastily. "Listen, we better get moving if you want to dive before the sun goes down. Are you both certified?"

"Yep, we've got our cards right here."

I took a look at the diving certification cards they each held out for me to inspect. Everything appeared to be in order.

"It'll be $50.00 a piece," I said. "We can leave whenever you're ready."

Normally I would have spent more time making small talk, but I didn't want them to ask me where I was from again. Will pulled out a $100.00 bill and handed it to Leon who put it in the register.

They gulped down the rest of their drinks and put their empty glasses on the bar. We walked down to the beach where I unlocked the shed and got out the diving equipment we would need. I gave them each a diving flashlight and a pair of fins. Then we suited up in weight belts, masks, air tanks, and snorkels. The snorkels would come in handy for the swim along the surface out into deeper water. It was clear that they did have at least some diving experience when they correctly waited until we entered the surf to put on their fins. They also wore their masks correctly by pushing them up from under their chins, instead of pulling them down from their foreheads.

As we swam out, I used my diving flashlight so I could see the ocean floor fall away below us. When I spotted the familiar coral reef I was looking for, I signaled to Steve and Will that we had reached our destination. We made a circle facing each other and treaded water as we prepared to dive.

First, we removed the snorkels from our mouths and let them float alongside our heads where they were attached by a strap. I watched Steve and Will carefully to make sure they inserted their air-tank's mouthpieces correctly. When I was confident that their tanks were working properly, we each added weights to our belts and began to sink below the ocean's surface.

When we reached a depth of fifty feet I signaled for them to follow me. I led them over the reef to where the wreck of the *Hanjin* waited on the other side. It lay like a sleeping giant at the bottom of the sea. For years the *Hanjin* had faithfully carried cargo to and from St. Thomas, but a fire broke out on her one day during one of her trips. When it became apparent that the fire would not be contained, the crew managed to evacuate, but the burning vessel did not sink. She had drifted, burning, for two days until the decision was finally made to sink her under gun-fire rather than let her come any closer to shore. The U.S Navy had gunned down the faithful ship until she finally succumbed in sixty feet of water. Now her wounded body served as a popular dive spot for tourists.

    I led them over the top of the wreck and along her exposed side. I ran my flashlight over her ghostly hull to reveal bullet holes the size of beer cans. Then I signaled them to follow me inside.

    We swam through the galley where the ship's cooking equipment was still largely intact. A jellyfish slowly drifted over the stove and an angelfish swam around the rusting refrigerator. We exited the wreck, and I treaded water while they swam around to explore the *Hanjin's* exterior further. I noticed a Hammerhead shark that swam nearby, but it didn't seem to be interested in us.

    I didn't like it, however, when I spotted a large, ominous shape that seemed to hang in the ocean further out. It was big enough to be a shark, but it didn't move like one. I took my eyes off of it to turn my attention back to my companions. Steve was examining a small octopus, but Will was nowhere to be seen. He came over the top of the *Hanjin* suddenly and I gave the hand signal to get them to follow me to the surface. As we ascended, I shone my flashlight on the ominous shape again. It had gotten close enough for me to see that it was a barracuda. It looked to be about five feet long. The three of us broke through ocean's surface almost in unison.

    "Jesus, that barracuda is huge!" Steve exclaimed as soon as he had taken his mouthpiece out of his mouth.

A small wave slapped his face and made a splat sound against his mask. He pulled it down beneath his chin as his body bobbed up and down in the rolling waves.

It's time we headed back," I said. I noticed that Will was wearing a silver necklace. "Take that off," I told him. "Barracudas are attracted to shiny things."

Will removed his necklace and appeared to put it in a pocket inside his swim trunks. I turned away from them and began swimming straight toward shore. Every so often I shone my flashlight back at the barracuda and each time it was a little closer.

I could see its strange, round head and its angry looking face. Even a casual scrape from its wiry teeth could deliver a fatal wound.

When I reached the first sandbar, I began swimming diagonally with the shore. I pointed my flashlight back at the barracuda again. It was further away this time. Finally, we made it into rougher surf which indicated that we were nearing the beach. Frothy waves tossed us around as we removed our fins and tiredly made our way out of the ocean.

Exhausted, we each stripped off our gear and tumbled onto the sand breathing heavily. Will fished his necklace out from his pocket and put it back around his neck. I lay back on the sand and stared up at the starlit night sky. After a few minutes, Steve interrupted our silence.

"Listen, we're going to a bar later," he said. "Want to meet us there?"

"Which one?" I asked.

"*Paradise Garage*. A French chick told us about it on the beach today."

I knew exactly who the French chick was that Steve was referring to.

"I know the place," I said. "Sure, I can meet you there in about an hour."

Steve and Will left so I began to stow the gear back inside the shed. When I finished, I found that Leon had shut the bar down for the night. I climbed onto my Triumph T120V Bonneville bike and headed home to get cleaned up. After a short ride up into the hills, I turned off the main road and drove through my poverty-stricken neighborhood. I pulled up in front of my small, faded blue bungalow that was surrounded by palm trees and rocky soil. It was constructed of thin, rotting wood except for the high, cement porch that had uneven wooden steps and no railing. There were no screens or glass in the windows, but that was O.K. because the climate was mild. There was always an ocean breeze blowing through the house. The electrical was faulty and I felt lucky when I had running water, but I lived there because my neighbors never asked any questions.

I parked my bike in my sloped front yard that flooded every time it rained. I waved at the kid who lived next door. He waved back and watched me as I went inside. I opened my warped wooden door and flipped on a light switch. The bulb that dangled at the end of a wire that hung suspended from the ceiling blinked to life. It illuminated the dust that covered the thin wooden walls and floors. Several iguanas went running for cover. I had no furniture except for a hammock I had hung up in the living room near the biggest window in the house. My kitchen didn't have a working stove or refrigerator, but what I really missed was a shower. The bathroom contained a rust-stained bathtub along with a small dingy sink and an old commode. The only good feature the house had was the view. Through the living room window I could see St. Thomas' deep-water harbor down below.

I walked through my empty bedroom and went into the bathroom to fill the tub. When I turned the spigot on brown, rust-colored water spewed out for several minutes before clear water came through. I hoped there would be hot water this time but no such luck. While the tub filled, I went into my closet and pulled out a clean shirt, jeans, and underwear. Fortunately, there was no place on the island that required more than casual clothing. I pulled off the t-shirt and shorts I was wearing and threw them on the floor.

Nude, I went back into the bathroom to examine myself in the short mirror above the sink. I had become someone I barely recognized. My skin, always prone to burning, had become darkly tanned from daily exposure to the sun. My reddish-blonde hair had become nearly white-blonde. I had always been in pretty good shape, but the daily kayaking trips and frequent dives had made me more lean and muscular than I had ever been before.

Bathing and dressing had taken only thirty minutes so I was soon back on my bike, headed toward downtown St. Thomas. There were only three bars that could be considered more than huts on a beach. Each one was devoted to a theme. The *Garage* was a disco, *Charlie's* was all about reggae and local musicians, and *Moonlight Mile* played rock like the Stones and the Beatles. I walked into the *Garage* and headed to the bar where I ordered a scotch on the rocks. My island friends had not been able to convince me to drink the sugary rum concoctions they preferred. I sipped my scotch and scanned the room for Steve or Will but saw no sign of them. I did, however, see the French chick who had invited them there. On the dance floor, Celine danced seductively with an older man who clumsily tried to follow her moves. I knew instantly that she had him on the line for an angle she was working.

"Well, would you look at that," Will said as he and Steve slid onto two barstools next to me. "I guess we didn't get here fast enough, fellas."

"I wouldn't take it too hard, guys," I said, "You never know what the night might bring."

After another dance with grandpa, Celine made her way over to the three of us.

"Boys," she said, "I see you made it. And you brought a friend." Her eyes met mine briefly. "Why are the three of you just sitting here with so many beautiful women around you? You should ask one of them to dance."

"We were hopin' to dance with you," Steve replied.

Celine's eyes narrowed like a cat's. "Aren't you just the sweetest man?" she cooed. Then she turned her attention to me.

"What about you?" she asked. "Do you want to dance with me, or aren't you the dancing type?"

"No ma'am," I responded. "Dancing is a bit fast for me. A lot of things are too fast for me."

I knew Celine could have breathed fire through her nostrils, but she smiled a frozen smile.

"Well, gentlemen, enjoy your evening," she said icily. "I have someone waiting for me."

She looked back over her shoulder and shot me a look that said *go to hell*.

"What's the matter with you?" Steve asked incredulously. "You should have danced with her! She was the reason we came here!"

"Consider yourselves lucky, boys," I replied, "That makes two barracudas you escaped from tonight."

I awakened the next morning to the sound of a Volkswagen Bug idling outside my house. The engine cut off, and then I heard the familiar "clomp, clomp, clomp" of platform sandals against my uneven wooden stairs. I swayed in my hammock as the thin wooden door to my house flew open.

"Que mal!" This place is a dump! You could live anywhere on the island but you live here, in a slum!"

I continued rocking in my hammock as Celine came around to face me.

"You bastard!" she yelled. "You use me to bring you clients and then you treat me like a whore! I don't know why I put up with you."

I reached out and grabbed her wrist hard. She tried to wrestle away, but I pulled her down on top of me onto the hammock. I kissed her while she struggled. She slapped me, but I only lifted her dress above her thighs and pushed myself into her. Her anger turned into ecstasy. When we finished we lay beside each other in the hammock. She lit a cigarette as we swayed together in silence. Finally, I had to ask.

"Who's the guy?"

"*Le grasa*! That pig! The things you make me do!"

"Is he buying or selling?"

"He's buying. And Mitch, I know how you feel about St. Martin, but Mitch, this is the deal of a lifetime! His name is Bates. He's a Texas oilman."

I got up off the hammock unceremoniously. My quick movement left her rocking too fast.

"Bastard!" she yelled as she gripped the hammock tightly to keep it from flipping over.

I walked into my bedroom without a reply. Our relationship consisted of her bitching and me ignoring her when I wasn't screwing her. I went into my bathroom and turned on the spigot at the sink so I could shave. After a few minutes, she appeared at the bathroom door wearing only her underwear and one of my t-shirts.

"Why do you live here?" she asked. "This house is awful and the neighborhood is a slum," she repeated.

"Feel free to get the hell out of here anytime you're ready," I retorted.

Usually, this would have been enough to send her stomping out. However, she changed gears which told me she wanted something.

"Look, Mitch, I don't want to fight with you today because you and I are going to be rich! Bates wants to buy *Le Luxueux!*"

Everyone in real estate on the islands knew about *Le Luxueux Hotel*. It was the most luxurious hotel on the island of St. Martin and it had been owned by the same family for generations. The family had fallen on hard times because of their baby brother's coke habit and needed to sell. Without the rest of the family realizing what he was doing, he had quit paying the hotel's bills and used the money to pay his drug and gambling debts instead. The rumor was that the family needed to unload it fast before the bank foreclosed. Whoever brokered the deal was sure to make a huge commission because the asking price was $2 million.

For anyone else in real estate brokering the sale of *Le Luxeux* would have been the deal of a lifetime, but for me there was a serious problem. The island of St. Martin was controlled by both the French and Dutch governments. I didn't have a license to do business there because I wasn't sure my forged identity documents would stand up under their scrutiny. I had consistently stayed away from doing business on St. Martin, but I had never told Celine the real reason why.

"I told you before," I said, "I'm not licensed on St. Martin and I don't know anything about French or Dutch real estate law. I'm not going to get involved in a real estate deal where I don't know the laws of the land."

"And I've told *you* before that I know French and Dutch real estate law," she cajoled. "I've done many deals on St. Martin. I can take care of everything. As for your license, I talked to Bates and he says not to worry about it."

"What does that mean?" I asked.

"He has connections in the government of St. Martin so he can fast-track your license approval. All you have to do is fill out the application."

"If he has connections in the government, then why the hell does he need us?" I asked.

"I said he has connections in the *government,* not in real estate. He needs the benefit of my considerable expertise," she said with a smug smile.

"Why don't you get the license then? I know you're not cutting me in on the commission out of the kindness of your heart."

She made a face at me in the bathroom mirror.

"I can't get a license because of a little incident that happened there a few years ago. I was arrested so they wouldn't approve me for a license if I applied."

"Bates can't make them overlook that?" I asked.

"I don't want him to know. Honestly Mitch, this is your lucky day, but you're acting like it's the worst thing that could happen!"

Just then one of the many iguanas that inhabited my house scurried into the bathroom.

"Degoutant!" she shouted as she scooted backward to get away from the lizard.

I ignored her fear of the iguana. If Bates could get the license for me and we did the deal together, I would be set for life. I owed it to myself to at least meet the man before I walked away.

"I'll meet Bates to discuss it, but I'm not committed," I told her casually.

"Come to his yacht tonight at eight o'clock," she said, her eyes still trained on the iguana. "It's called the *Pure Lady.*"

"That makes one of you," I told her.

"Imbecile!" she shouted.

She stomped back through the bedroom. I heard her rustle around in the living room as she gathered her clothes and got dressed. The front door to my house slammed and then I heard the "clomp, clomp" sound of her heels again as she made her way down the porch steps. The engine of her VW roared to life and she was gone.

Chapter 14
St. Thomas, U.S. Virgin Islands, March, 1979

The deep water harbor near downtown St. Thomas was dotted with stream-lined, luxurious yachts. They floated against a backdrop of moonlight and purplish volcanic mountains. As I parked my bike and took in the view, I couldn't help but remember Harbor Town on the night of the shrimp festival. I walked down the dimly lit dock to where a dark-headed, gangly boy of thirteen waited in a dinghy to take me out to the *Pure Lady*. I was skeptical when I saw how young he was, but his skill became obvious when he began to expertly guide the tiny boat out toward the huge yacht. The full moon overhead lit the deep, dark water in patches so that it looked silvery in some spots and black in others. The familiar sight of yachts in a harbor brought up memories I had tried to forget. While the kid rowed, I stared down into the deep water and thought about Mia lying dead in her grave and the *Polargo* lying somewhere at the bottom of the Atlantic Ocean.

I snapped out of it as we drew near the *Pure Lady*. She was impressive at one hundred feet. She was moored further out because of her size and her commanding presence seemed to reign over the other yachts. We came along her starboard side and then the kid steered us around to her aft deck where two motorized boats were tied. He held the dinghy steady as he guided it over to an aluminum ladder.

"I see you've done this a few times before, huh kid?" I asked him.

He nodded and gave me a wide smile. I grabbed hold of the ladder, stepped off the dinghy, and climbed aboard. Almost as soon as I made it on deck, I felt like I shouldn't have come. I had a bad feeling, but I didn't have time to dwell on it. A tall, balding man in a tuxedo was waiting for me.

"This way, Mr. Jordanger," he said in a prim, English accent.

He led me along the *Pure Lady's* stark white deck beneath warm, amber lights. They cast gold shadows along the wall and across the man's bald head as he walked in front of me. After a few minutes, he stopped at a sliding glass door and slid it open. He then pulled back a filmy, tan curtain and I saw Bates and Celine inside. Bates stood behind a beautifully polished bar. I recognized that it was made from teak because of Delphine's infamous tour. Celine lounged against the bar. Her back was to me.

Bates gave me a friendly smile when he saw me and came out from behind the bar. When he reached me he stuck out his hand and shook mine vigorously. He wore a loud Hawaiian print shirt with white pants and brown deck shoes. Celine wore a tight black dress that revealed her tanned shoulders. She sat down on one of the barstools and watched me and Bates with a cold look in her eyes. I figured she was still mad about the fight we had earlier, but I couldn't help noticing that she looked good.

"How was your trip out, Mr. Jordanger? Elvis took good care of you?" Bates asked.

"Yes, he did just fine," I said. "He's steady with a boat."

"He should be," Bates replied, "Elvis has worked on this yacht since he was eight years old. My wife and I adopted him on a trip to Laos."

Bates paused and turned to the man in the tuxedo. "That will be all, Ackerley," he said.

Ackerley turned on his heel and left the room.

"Elvis' parents had died and well, it just seemed like the right thing to do," Bates continued. "My wife is a huge Elvis Presley fan, so she named the kid after him."

I nodded and looked around the room. A streamlined sofa with a bright, yellow and black geometric pattern sat facing the large sliding glass door through which I had entered. A carved bookshelf lined the wall behind it. A black chandelier made of wrought iron balls hung in the center of the room. Large, panoramic windows provided a three hundred sixty degree view of the Caribbean ocean and huge volcanic mountains out in the distance.

"Can I get you a drink, Mr. Jordanger? Celine said you like scotch, is that right?" Bates asked. He was already making his way back toward the bar.

"Call me Mitch and yes, scotch would be great," I said as I followed him.

I leaned against the bar next to Celine and watched Bates as he poured my drink. When he finished he handed the glass to me. I took a long swig of the smooth liquor.

"This is good stuff," I said. "It's hard to find good scotch on the island."

"Yes," Bates replied as he filled another glass with ice. "I've noticed that myself. Rum seems to be the liquor of choice here."

"You boys ready to talk about *Le Luxueux*?" Celine asked. She looked at us with a mixture of boredom and mild annoyance.

Bates laughed and winked at Celine. He seemed to be a good-natured guy, so I felt a little sorry for him because of what Celine had in store. I had seen her play her games with rich men many times before. She would string them along until they dropped some serious cash on her. Then she would send them home to their wives, humiliated and broken-hearted.

"Celine is eager for me to buy the hotel," Bates chuckled. "What do you know about it, Mitch?"

"The owners are asking $2 million but they need to sell fast. I would offer $1.2 and negotiate from there."

"Yes, that's what Celine said as well. It seems that I'm in good hands with the two of you," he said.

"Celine said you could fast-track a license for me," I said.

"Well, yes, through the Dutch licensing bureau, that is. It so happens that the man who runs it is an old family friend. As soon as you send in your paperwork, he's agreed to put your application at the top of the pile. Unfortunately, I don't know anyone who can help you on the French side."

My pulse began to race and my hands felt clammy. I knew this had been a mistake. Damn Celine and her greed. She had lied to me! I wanted to knock her off her barstool. I looked over at her, but she wouldn't look at me. She stared down into the drink Bates had made for her.

"Well, Mr. Bates," I said, "I don't think I'm qualified to guide you through this purchase. I don't know French or Dutch real estate law, and I've never even seen *Le Lexueux*."

Bates looked confused and Celine shot me a look. She had expected me to help her convince Bates to buy the hotel and hire us as his real estate agents. Normally, I would have gladly played the part of the supreme real estate expert just like I played the part of the humble, island tour guide. But this time it was too risky. I wasn't going to go along.

"You've never *seen* the hotel in *person?*" Bates asked as he poured himself another drink.

I could feel Celine's tension as she glared at me from her barstool, but I had made my decision. I had come to the *Pure Lady* hoping Bates was the kind of guy who cut corners like Sonny did back home. I had hoped he would overlook a few things about me if he were to find them out, and maybe even protect me if the governments of St. Martin exposed me as a fraud. But now that I had met Bates in person, I knew he was an honest man. I couldn't go into business with him using a fake identity.

"No, Mr. Bates, I haven't. Celine may not have told you, but I'm not going to be involved in this deal."

I was sure Celine was repressing a very strong urge to rake her nails across my face. I was bowing out and by doing so I was taking away the deal of a lifetime. Without me, Celine was sunk. She couldn't get a license either.

"No, Celine did **not** tell me that," Bates said as he looked at her pointedly. "I appreciate your honesty, Mr. Jordanger, but I didn't realize we were negotiating your agency's involvement. Let's say you change your mind and decide to be involved, what can you offer me?"

"Only the information I've already given you, and a recommendation that you have your own attorney review the chain of title. You don't want any liens to attach after the property comes out of escrow."

Bates blinked at me. "It seems like you could be a big help to me, after all," he said. "Surely 7% of $1.5 million is enough to entice you?"

I hesitated. I wanted the money and I had never shied away from taking a risk before. However, I had never lived under a fake name with a murder hanging over my head before, either.

"I'm sorry," I said, "I wouldn't feel right about it. *Le Lexueux* is outside my area of expertise." My voice sounded wooden as I said the words. I was sure Bates knew I was lying.

"Mitch, you're being ridiculous!" Celine interrupted. "Dennis, let me talk to him alone," she pleaded.

"That won't be necessary," I told her.

Bates looked skeptical, but he put his drink down on the bar and extended his hand to shake mine again.

"Then I guess there's nothing more to say," he said. "I thought you were trying to drive up your fee, but I see that's not the case."

He pressed a button on a control panel behind the bar. The man in the tuxedo reappeared at the sliding glass door almost immediately.

"Ackerley will show you out and Elvis will take you ashore," he said. "I'm sorry we won't be doing business together, Mr. Jordanger."

I avoided looking at Celine as I put my drink down on the bar. I got up from my barstool and walked over to where Ackerley waited for me. He slid the glass door open again and held the sheer curtain back so I could step through the doorway. He was about to slide the door closed behind me when Bates called my name once more.

"Mr. Jordanger," he said with narrowed eyes, "I must say that you've aroused my curiosity. I never met a businessman who turned down money before."

When Elvis had dropped me back on shore, I paced along the dock nervously and stopped at intervals to look back at the *Pure Lady*. If Bates looked into my personal business, he might find out things I didn't want known. Damn Celine for lying to me! She had made it sound like the license was in the bag. I had believed her because I wanted to. My gut had told me to stay away from this deal, but I had listened to my greed instead.

Bates probably had someone investigating me already. He would soon find out that I wasn't Mitchell Jordanger. I was Martin Richard McCloud, wanted in Louisiana for the murder of Delphine Perry. He might also discover that when I left Hilton Head, I stole $100,000.00 from Eric, Vince, and Dave. I had taken the money from the band's bank account and I still had most of it with me. It was my nest-egg so I could start over. It was all the money I had and another reason I didn't want to be found. If Eric heard that I was alive, he would crucify me if he got the chance. He had been right to accuse me of stealing over the years. I took a little from the account from time to time, and got kickbacks from club owners that the guys never knew about. I did it because I felt like I was entitled to a bigger share. I was the one who worked to get us a record deal while Eric held us back. Vince and Dave never stood up to Eric so they didn't have any of the headaches like I did. They were content to ride along.

A loud banging sound followed by angry profanity interrupted my thoughts. Startled, I walked over to the edge of the dock and looked down over the railing. An elderly, drunken man sat shakily in an old, tattered row boat. His skin was darkly tanned and he sported a long, straggly beard. His tattered clothes hung loosely over his emaciated body. He was cursing angrily because his boat had gotten tangled up with the one next to it. He kept banging on it to get loose. It would have been easy for him to row out a little and get free, but he was so drunk that he didn't realize it.

"You son of a bitch!" he screamed as he banged on the boat with his oar.

I watched him like a scientist watches a lab-rat while he tried to get out of his predicament. He kept banging on the boat until quite by accident he got free. At first he didn't realize he was free, but then instinct must have kicked in because he started rowing like a pro. I was impressed with his ability, but he was in a lot of danger. He was heading out into very deep, shark-infested water and he was so drunk that he couldn't see. It was only a matter of time before he capsized. When he did, there would be no way for him to find his boat in the darkness. If I didn't help him he was going to drown, or else something even worse was going to happen to him.

To my complete surprise, he made it as far as where the first yacht was moored in the harbor. I watched with fascination when he started swinging at its ropes with his oar. He flailed dangerously as he swung and nearly capsized. I couldn't believe it. It didn't even seem real. This man had put himself in a very dangerous situation, and I was the only person on earth who knew.

He finally quit banging on the rope and paddled further out, presumably to attack another yacht. After a while, I couldn't see him, but I could still hear him shouting profanity into the night sky. After a few more minutes, I couldn't hear him anymore. I took a long look at the small fishing boat he had abused. I could take it and go get him. He couldn't have gotten very far.

Strangely, I was reminded of a dream I had on the beach in Corpus Christie just before Eve disappeared. The dock, the deep water, and the man's crazy predicament had brought it all back. In the dream, Mia wanted me to save a gull that had broken its wing. It had flailed in deep water to keep from drowning. What was it that I said to Mia? Oh yes, *better let nature take its course*. I turned away from the harbor and walked over to my bike. I got on and drove home without another look back.

Chapter 15
St. Thomas, U.S. Virgin Islands, March, 1979

It was a sunny day in Hilton Head. Gulls squawked loudly as they flew over where Mia and I floated on the Polargo in Sea Pines Cove. She smiled at me as she raised her glass to make a toast. I smiled back at her and raised my glass as well.

"To us," she said happily.

"To us," I replied.

"To the dead baby," she said, still smiling.

"To the dead baby?" I asked.

"You killed it," she said. She took a long, celebratory sip from her glass and put it on the table in front of her. "Now I'll just go into the water and see if it needs anything."

I awoke with a start in my hammock and sent two iguanas scurrying along my window sill. What had Mia been saying to me in the dream? Christ, she'd seemed so real. If she had lived, everything would have been different. I missed her.

I sat up in the hammock slowly and pulled my sweaty t-shirt away from my body. As I looked around at the dusty room, the events from last night began to replay in my mind. The drunken man in the tiny row boat had certainly drowned or become shark bait after I left the harbor last night. Mia would have rescued him if she had been there, but unfortunately for him, I was there instead. Something inside me had snapped when I watched him row out to sea. I was reminded of how good it felt to be empowered with life and death decisions. I felt like a king deciding the fate of one of his subjects. The urge to kill had been asleep inside me like a disease in temporary remission, but now it was awake once more. I had denied my urges so I could be with Mia, but she was gone and there was no use denying them anymore. I was a killer, but to keep from getting caught I would have to plan things out. I would choose anonymous, inconsequential people who were completely unrelated to me. I would dispose of them just like a vulture disposes of road kill.

Unfortunately for me, Bates wasn't the least bit inconsequential and that was exactly why I had to kill him. He was a rich, powerful man who had a stable of lawyers at his beck and call. He probably had them start investigating me before Elvis had even dropped me off back at the dock. He would soon find out that I was wanted in Louisiana for murder, that I was living under an alias, and that I had stolen $100,000.00 from my friends. He would probably tell Celine what he knew, so I was going to have to kill her as well.

The sun set at 8:00 p.m. and left the road I was taking to the beach in almost complete darkness. I could have taken an easier, well lit drive down to the dock at the harbor but I wasn't going to approach the *Pure Lady* from there. I had decided I would kayak to her from a secluded beach located on the other side of the volcanic mountains. I had relied on my kayak on the night I sank the *Polargo*, and I would rely on it again tonight so I could get to Bates and kill him.

The trip out to the yacht was easy because the water was as smooth as glass. It was nothing like the Atlantic was on the night

Karen Oliver

I paddled through rough, white-capped waves to Sonny's restaurant on the marsh. I was barely breathing hard when I spotted the *Pure Lady* within swimming distance. I dropped anchor and slid off the side of the kayak quietly. I began to swim toward the *Pure Lady* as quickly as I could because of all the sharks that I knew were patrolling the area. When I reached the aluminum ladder Elvis had taken me to the night before, I grabbed onto it and climbed aboard. On deck, I spotted an oar that was hanging from a hook. I took it down and carried it with me in case I needed to kill Bates with it, or anyone else that I might run into. With the oar in hand, I dripped water all along the deck as I made my way to the salon where I'd had a drink with Bates and Celine the night before.

It was my good fortune to surprise him as he stepped through the salon's sliding glass doors. I swung the oar hard and made contact with his forehead before he knew what was happening. Blood spurted out and his knees buckled. As he went down, he tried to grab onto the *Pure Lady's* railing for help, but I hit him again on the side of his skull. His head looked crushed and open like a tomato that had been dropped on a super-market floor. He slumped down onto the deck beside the rail and moved no more. It was obvious that he was dead.

At that moment, I heard a woman's voice coming from inside the salon. The voice was muffled but I knew at once that it was Celine. I hastily pulled Bates' heavy body up from the deck and then hoisted it over the *Pure Lady's* side. His heavy, clumsy body made a loud splash when it hit the water some ten feet below deck. I was sure Celine had heard it and figured she was on her way outside. This was my chance to kill her. I picked up the bloody oar and waited for her to step through the sliding glass doors. Suddenly the whole yacht seemed to come alive with people who were on the alert. I had to get out of there fast. I threw the oar over-board and heard it make another splash. Then I swung my legs over the rail and jumped. As I fell away from the *Pure Lady*, I contorted my body into the straightest line possible. I hoped that when I entered the water, there wouldn't be a sound.

It felt like I sank thirty feet when I went under. I swam for the surface thinking I would never find it. The water was full of blood. The sharks that regularly swam through the area to scavenge leftover dinners thrown overboard from the yachts would quickly be attracted. I thought of this and of Bates, who was somewhere down there with me. After an interminable time struggling to reach the surface, I broke through and swam like an Olympian toward my kayak. The thought of sharks at my ankles and Bates at my legs kept me moving faster than I had ever moved in my entire life. I reached my kayak and grabbed it so I could slide my torso onto it, but when I did I felt a searing pain tear through my lower back. I must have injured it when I threw Bates over. Lights were coming on back at the *Pure Lady*. Someone had a spotlight and was feverishly searching the water where Bates and I had gone over. I could not afford to be seen in that light. Despite the pain, I pulled myself onto the kayak and then paddled with all my strength back toward the beach.

***

Two months went by before I saw Celine again. I had spent most of that time recuperating from my back injury, so it was a coincidence that I was at *Jimmy's* on the day she came. I was getting the boating gear ready for another group of tourists when she walked up to me on the beach. The white linen top she wore made a nice contrast against her tan skin. She stared up at me from behind over-sized sunglasses while the ocean breeze blew her chestnut hair around her face. Even though she wore the glasses, I could tell that she was scared.

"The police are ruling Dennis' death a suicide," she said.

She seemed to want me to say something about it, but I didn't. After a few minutes of silence, she pulled her sunglasses off in exasperation. There were dark circles under her eyes. She looked like she hadn't slept in weeks.

"There was so much blood and water on the deck of the *Pure Lady*," she said, "and Elvis told them he saw a man throw something over and then jump. But they will have none of it."

She paused as her eyes desperately searched my face. I still said nothing so she continued.

"I would have come to your house to tell you this, Mitch," she said weakly, "only…..I don't think I want to be alone with you anymore."

She kept staring at me like a frightened animal. She wanted me to deny that I had killed Bates. That way she could go on fighting, scheming, and sleeping with me without the horrible knowledge that I was a monster. But I couldn't do it. Her lie was the reason I had to kill Bates in the first place. I sure as hell wasn't going to make her feel good about it. I gave her a look that confirmed her worst fears.

She covered her mouth with her hands and shook her head softly. Tears sprang into her eyes as she backed away from me on the beach. When she got a few feet away from me, she turned around and ran. I watched her go knowing that I would never see her again.

I heard later that she had moved to St. Martin. I knew she would do well there because she had always known French and Dutch real estate law just as she had claimed. In the small, close knit community of St. Thomas locals, news of her departure had traveled fast. Maybe I was paranoid, but it seemed that the reason she'd left had traveled fast as well. Whenever I drank in the local bars, I was avoided by the very same people who used to buy me a scotch on sight. I began to go out less and I spent most of my time alone. I got so lonely that I started looking forward to the company of the tourists who came to *Jimmy's*. As word got around about Bates, my real estate business began to suffer. The tours and the bar still did well, though, because I continued to send kick-backs to the right people. These people only wanted their money. They weren't the least bit interested in what happened to Bates.

Leon and Marquita, however, each signaled their disapproval in their own way. Leon disappeared for good, but Marquita was forced to continue to bring tourist groups to me because she worked for one of the hotels I had bribed. In defiance, though, she no longer let me know when a group had arrived. She would deposit them at the bar without a word to me. I'd learned to pay attention to the time in order to avoid getting low tips from aggravated tourists who'd been left waiting.

One evening, I decided to have a drink at the *Paradise Garage* even though I knew I wouldn't be welcome. I sat alone at the bar while Sandro, the bartender I'd given money to once when his mother was sick, barely spoke to me. I sipped my scotch on the rocks and stared straight ahead.

I had gotten used to being ignored, so imagine my surprise when I overheard a man's voice ask Sandro if he knew me. Only he wasn't asking about *Mitchell Jordanger*. He was asking about *Martin Richard McCloud*. I looked over at the man carefully from out of the corner of my eye. He looked like he had just arrived on the island. He was pale, clean shaven, and over-dressed. His beige pants and white dress shirt were both stained with sweat. He mopped his brow as he took out a photo of me with darker hair and paler skin. He leaned on the bar as he showed it to Sandro.

Sandro took the photo and pretended to look at it as he tried not to glance in my direction. He wasn't my friend anymore, but it seemed he didn't want to rat me out to a stranger. I had become a pariah in the community, but apparently I still rated higher than a *tourist*. Sandro shook his head and handed the photo back to the pale man. I sucked in my breath as the man started to look over in my direction. He seemed to think better of it, though, because he stopped and plopped himself down onto a barstool.

"Can I get a rum and coke?" he asked.

Sandro nodded and began to make the drink. The stranger loosened his tie and slumped forward onto the bar with both elbows. "Jesus, it's hot here, ya know?"

Sandro nodded and kept his eyes on the activity of preparing the drink. I could tell he was moving slowly in order to allow me time to leave without being noticed. I took my cue. I put a $20.00 down on the bar, far more than enough to cover my one scotch on the rocks, and slid off my barstool. When I stood up, the man started to look my way. Sandro diverted his attention with a question.

"Why are you looking for this Martin McCloud? Who is he?"

It wasn't the question I might have hoped Sandro would ask, but it kept the stranger from looking over at me.

"He inherited some money," the stranger replied smugly. "I was hired to find him, so he can claim it."

Sandro and I both knew the story was bullshit. It was an old line people used when they wanted to flush someone out. At least the lie made Sandro more determined to help me, because he was very determined not to help a *lying tourist*.

"Wow," Sandro replied in an effort to play along. "How much money is it?"

The stranger was encouraged by Sandro's wide-eyed, island native act.

"It's a lot," he said enthusiastically. "More than most people would need for a lifetime. But if I don't find him soon, the money's gonna go to the next person in line."

What a lie! I nodded at Sandro and mouthed the word, "thanks".

I left the bar and sped back home. While I furiously packed my belongings, I obsessed about the guy. Who was he? Why was he looking for me? He would have flashed a badge if he was a federal agent or a police officer, so he had to be a private detective. As I threw the last few articles of clothing into my bag, I wondered who had sent him. Maybe Bates found out who I was before I killed him. But if he did, he wouldn't need to send a private detective to look for me. He could have the cops pick me up with the proof he would have had. Celine wouldn't have sent him, either. She knew where I lived.

The only other people who knew I was in St. Thomas were Sonny and Mike. But they wouldn't send a guy to find Martin McCloud when they knew I was using the alias they gave me. Whoever it was who sent him, they were chasing me out of St. Thomas and I didn't like it one bit. I was leaving behind my houses, the bar, and the real estate and tourism businesses. I could only hope that I would be back to claim them again one day.

Chapter 16
Mobile, Alabama, November, 2007

"Mitch, get my make-up bag for me. I packed it and then left it on the vanity. Please bring it with you."

Melanie was calling me from her car on her way to the Atlanta airport. She was about to fly to Mobile, Alabama. I planned to meet her there tomorrow after I got off work. I had stayed behind to finish a security surveillance project for *Wilson's* and that was lucky because as usual she had forgotten something. Mobile was the town we were going to spend Thanksgiving in this year, and as long as everything went well, Mobile was going to lose one of its less upstanding citizens on this holiday. I had already packed everything I would need. The duct tape, the empty water bottle, plastic bags, paper towel, and the cheap shoes that were one size too big would all go with me in my suitcase. As usual, I would buy some bleach and water for the clean-up after I landed. I never packed the liquids so I could avoid any static from airport security. Since Melanie and I were arriving separately, I hoped to buy the bleach and water and still have time to hunt, kill, and dispose of an "inconsequential" before I met her at the motel. Mobile was a little closer to my home in Atlanta than I liked, but I wasn't deterred. I was counting on the fact that no one knew me there and the quick nature of my visit to keep my identity concealed. So long as I wasn't seen and the person I killed was completely unrelated to me, there should be no reason for the police to connect me to their disappearance.

I left *Wilson's* on a Wednesday afternoon and went home to spend the night before Thanksgiving alone. I was glad to have some time to myself before the challenge I would face tomorrow night. I slept unusually well and awoke on the morning of November 22nd refreshed and eager to go. I felt strangely awake as I drove the familiar, now deserted streets to the Atlanta airport to board an empty plane. Almost everyone else had already traveled to be with their families so the airport was oddly quiet. I liked it when things were like this. The world seemed like my personal universe where time stood still.

The flight from Atlanta to Mobile took just under an hour. Everything was going as planned until I got to the airport car rental office. The car they gave me was a sky blue Nissan Pathfinder. The color was flashier than I liked for my purposes, but it was the only car they had because of the holiday. I reluctantly threw my bag into the back of it and climbed inside. As I did so, I noticed that the temperature in Mobile was warmer than it had been in Atlanta, but it was still cool at fifty-three degrees. Melanie was waiting for me in a motel room off Airport Boulevard and I-65, but I wasn't going there just yet. It had been a year since I had stalked my prey, and I was eager to do it again.

I pulled through a Shell gas station that shared a parking lot with a Block-Buster video store and waited to assess the locals. Through the store's large windows, I watched a middle-eastern man who worked as the cashier debate with an under-aged girl who was trying to buy beer. She didn't fit the profile of the person I was hunting. She was young and hadn't given up on life yet.

I was looking for an empty, burned out person who would call to me with their loneliness and misery. I watched the melodrama play out inside the store for a few more minutes. I finally got so bored that I decided to move on.

I pulled off from the convenience store and headed north on Airport Blvd. At the intersection of Airport and University, three orange cones blocked one of the lanes of the four lane highway. When the light turned green, I went around the cones by simply changing lanes. I drove by them slowly until I came upon a heavy-set cop who vigorously waved me down. As I pulled over, I saw that his meaty face was red with anger.

"Boy, didn't you see that police road-block back there? Let me see your license, BOY!"

I didn't know what the hell road-block he was talking about but I handed him my license. He looked at it and then took it with him as he walked to the rear of the car and looked at my plate.

"Atlanta, huh?" he asked sarcastically when he came back to my car window and handed my license back. "Well, you Yankees may drive like idiots up there but down here we DO NOT CROSS A POLICE BARRICADE!!!!" he screamed. "We've got a busted water main up here. You turn this vehicle around and get the HELL OUT OF HERE!!!!!"

He turned his mammoth frame on his heel and stomped away.

Prick, I thought. *In Atlanta we can afford real road-block equipment instead of three little orange cones in one lane of the highway.*

I was pissed because the ignorant cop had called me "boy" and bawled me out, but I was **_seething_** because my plans for Thanksgiving were ruined. I couldn't kill anyone now because the cop had identified me. He could connect me with my rental car. It was just the kind of chance incident I couldn't afford.

I was too angry to go and sit in a motel room with Melanie, so I decided to drive downtown to re-visit some antebellum neighborhoods I had admired in the past. In my former life, the Henley-McCloud Band had played at *Trinity's Bar* on the outskirts of the neighborhoods, and I had always thought they were beautiful. On my way downtown, I passed a bar that looked open so I decided to stop for a drink. I pulled into a parking lot across the street from it and parked under a Magnolia tree.

The bar was located inside a building that looked like an old department store from the late 50s or early 60s. A big display window was outlined with a string of soft, white Christmas lights and someone had spray-painted the corners of it with fake snow. "Wintzell's Bar" was stenciled in the middle of the window in big, black letters. Next to the display window was an old-fashioned looking revolving door. I pushed on the door and walked inside where I found myself face to face with a wooden wall. It forced me to go to the right in order to access the bar any further. When I came around the wall, I saw booths made of thick, carved wood and a long bar that ran down the center of the room. Beyond the bar, a stage and some tables and chairs filled in the view. A woman with long straight, light-brown hair sat atop a stool alone on stage. Over-head lights revealed the dust that was in the air. It floated around her as she played a guitar and sang Fleetwood Mac's "Landslide". There weren't a lot of people in the bar but I supposed that was to be expected since it was the evening of Thanksgiving Day.

"What'll ya have?" a young bartender asked as I slid onto a barstool. He was heavy-set and had swarthy skin and jet-black hair.

"Scotch on the rocks; thanks."

I turned back toward the stage where the woman was finishing her song to light applause. I noticed a man I'd overlooked before who sat close to the stage. He was clapping his hands enthusiastically. The woman smiled and stood up as she slid her guitar strap over her head. She walked over to the man and took his outstretched hand as she descended a small staircase that led from the stage down to the bar. I continued to watch them as they made their way over to where I was sitting. The man was much older than the woman. He appeared to be around my age, but she couldn't have been more than twenty-eight. He wore a white button down shirt with jeans and a cowboy hat. She looked like a hippie in a black, long-sleeved t-shirt and bell bottom jeans. The man seemed to be enamored with the woman, while she appeared to tolerate his attention politely. Just before they reached the bar, she handed her guitar to him and headed off somewhere. For a moment he looked like he might follow her, but he turned back to the bar and continued toward us instead.

"Johnny, get me the usual!" the cowboy called out to the dark-haired kid behind the bar. It struck me that his voice sounded very familiar. He took a seat next to me and propped the guitar up against the bar. After a minute the bartender slid a frosty mug of beer over to him.

"Connie was real good tonight," the bartender said with admiration. He wiped up some beer that had spilled when he slid the mug to the cowboy.

"Yep, she's going out on the road soon," the familiar voice replied. "We're heading to Baton Rouge after Christmas."

A fat, cigar-smoking man at the other end of the bar adjusted his heavy frame on his barstool. He rotated around so that he faced the cowboy. "We sure appreciate you and Connie coming out on Thanksgiving to play for us," he said.

"Wintzie, your place is like a home away from home for me and Connie. We'd rather play here than anywhere else."

"Wintzie" must be the owner of Wintzell's Bar, I thought.

The Darkness Behind the Door

They raised their mugs to each other and took long swigs of their beers. I listened intently as they continued their friendly conversation. Every time the cowboy spoke electricity shot through me. My jaws were clinched with recognition and surprise. After a while, the singer reappeared and told the cowboy she was ready to leave. Anticipation made the hair on the back of my neck stand up because he was about to walk right by me. He guzzled his beer and then picked up the guitar. I studied the bottom of my glass as they moved past me so he wouldn't see my face. They walked by me without a break in their strides. He was interested only in her. There had been no flicker of recognition on his part that I could see. I put down more than enough money to pay for my drink and hurriedly followed them to the revolving door. I watched them through the big department store window as they got into a red pick-up truck. After they pulled away from the curb, I dashed across the street to the Pathfinder and then drove like a maniac until I caught up to them. I tried to stay back at a reasonable distance so they wouldn't realize they were being followed.

The cowboy's pick-up turned down one dimly lit street after another but in the end we only went a few blocks. He'd had to wind around because of all the one-way streets in the downtown area. Finally, he pulled up in front of a clapboard style house where a front porch light blazed over a dingy screen door. The woman, Connie, got out of the passenger side door with her guitar slung over one shoulder. She walked determinedly toward the house as if she was afraid that the cowboy would follow her. When she reached the house she didn't go inside the front door. Instead, she went to a set of rickety wooden steps that led to an apartment over the garage. When she reached the mid-way point on the staircase, she turned back toward the truck and waved.

Now that must have pissed him off, I thought. No goodnight kiss.

Karen Oliver

She reached the top of the stairs and went inside the apartment. A light went on inside and Connie's form could be seen moving about. The truck sat where it was for several minutes before it finally pulled away. I followed it as it led me to a seedy area I wasn't familiar with. At last, the truck turned into the broken paved driveway of a small shop. On one of the shop's whitewashed walls, the word *pawn* was scrolled in faded, black cursive. I turned down a side street while the cowboy parked his truck. I watched in my rearview mirror as he got out and walked inside.

I drove down the side street a little further and parked next to an empty field of over-grown grass and weeds. I turned off the Pathfinder's interior light before I opened the car door so I wouldn't be spotted when I got out. There weren't any street lights, so I was able to walk from my car to the pawn shop in almost total darkness. Unfortunately, the pawn shop was a freestanding building so every side of it was exposed to the street. I tried to stay in the shadows as I made my way around to the door that the cowboy had gone into. To my surprise, I found that it was unlocked. I pushed it open slowly and carefully stepped inside. The room was pitch-black so it took a minute for my eyes to adjust. Gradually, I was able to see a pathway in front of me with large glass display cases on either side. There was no sign of the cowboy anywhere. I walked toward the back of the store taking care not to knock anything over or set off an alarm. When I got to the back I still didn't see the cowboy. He seemed to have disappeared into a mist.

There were two doors in the back of the shop. According to the signs on the doors, one was a bathroom and the other was an office. The bathroom door was slightly ajar so I could see that it was empty. I gently pushed on the door to the office and stepped inside. As my sight began to adjust to this new, darker room I heard a click. The soft light of a banker's lamp illuminated the room and revealed the cowboy. He was sitting behind a desk. He looked me over and then reclined back in his chair. I saw the double-barrel shotgun he held. It was pointed directly at my chest.

"Well, well," he said deliberately. "It **is** you. I must say it took my mind some convincin' when I saw you at *Wintzell's* tonight. But then, I never did believe you killed yourself by sinking that houseboat."

"I wondered if you grieved any," I returned. "I never knew if you and I really hated each other, or if we really loved each other."

"Do people who love you steal your money?" Eric asked sarcastically. "Or is that why you came here tonight? You came here to give me back my share of the money that you stole from me, Dave, and Vince. Is that it?"

"Well, I didn't come here to kill you, Eric," I said as I nodded at the shotgun.

"Maybe you did and maybe you didn't," Eric said. He leaned forward with the gun and placed his elbows on his desk. "But I know what you're capable of, Marty, so I'm not taking any chances. You showed us all what a cold-hearted, psychotic bastard you are when you killed that girl and took our money."

"I didn't kill Mia," I said flatly.

"I'm really not interested, old buddy," Eric retorted. "That poor girl's fate was sealed on the day she met you. All I care about now is the money. I want to know where it is. For your sake, you better be able to get it for me."

"Eric, please try and understand," I pleaded. "I had to take that money so I could start over. I didn't kill Mia, but I did kill someone else. They had it coming, but someone saw me do it. I had to disappear before the police arrested me."

I didn't expect Eric to understand or give a damn about why I stole his money, but I had to keep him talking until I could get the gun away from him.

"That didn't give you the right to steal from us, Marty!" Eric sneered. "My God, you are **unbelievable**! You think everything you do is *justified*, somehow! Do you have any idea what you did to Vince and Dave when you pretended to drown and took all the money they had? Not that you give a damn, you son of a bitch, but Vince was so devastated by your death that he eventually O.D.'d. He over-dosed because of **you**, you bastard! You were like a brother to him, you see, so he blamed himself when he thought you committed suicide. I tried to tell him, but he never believed what a selfish, psychotic bastard you are. And Dave? Well, Dave finally believed what I had been saying all along when we went to pay for your funeral and found out our money was gone. But by then it was too late because without you and Vince, the band fell apart. He didn't have the money you stole to fall back on, so he was barely able to support Jill and Eve. I tried to help him, but he refused to take any money from me. He went on to struggle as a bartender at one gig after another. But none of that matters to you, does it?"

"I didn't mean to hurt any of you, Eric. I was just a scared kid. I never could have imagined that my disappearance would affect you guys the way it did. You always told me you didn't need me in the band to make it anyway."

I took a step closer to him, but he noticed what I did. He cocked the trigger on the shotgun.

"Save it," he said. "I'm only going to ask you one more time. Where is the money that you stole from us?"

"I took it to St. Thomas with me," I said quickly.

A strange look crossed Eric's face. He released his grip on the shotgun for a second. I quickly sat down on an armchair that was placed across from where he sat behind his desk.

"Don't move!" Eric commanded as he re-tightened his grip on the gun.

I froze. Now that I was closer to him, I was able to take a good look at his face. He was definitely older than I remembered but overall he'd held up well. He was still lean and muscular, but the wisps of hair that poked out from under his cowboy hat were completely gray. I could also see that he was very drunk. He seemed to be getting tired from holding the gun. He was starting to let it sway a little when he talked.

"St. Thomas, huh?" he mused. "Well, well. I sent someone out there to look for you, but they didn't find you."

"You sent someone to *St. Thomas*?" I asked incredulously. "How did you know I was there?"

"You have a lot of enemies, Marty. Someone tipped me off. Seems they wanted you dead just as much as I did." He let the gun sway again before he continued. "I wanted to get our money back mostly so I could give it to Dave, and I wanted to kill you for taking it in the first place. I never found you back then, but lucky for me, it looks like I'm going to get my revenge after all."

"I've still got the money, Eric," I cajoled. "I can get it for you in the morning."

"Keep it," he slurred. "After Vince died, I offered twice the amount you stole to that Italian bastard you were so chummy with. I wanted him to hunt you down and kill you. He wouldn't talk to me when I went to see him at his bar but his guard dog, Mike, walked me to my car. He told me to go home and check my mail. I didn't know what the hell he was talking about but the next day, there was a single piece of paper lying inside my mailbox. *St. Thomas* was written on it. I sent someone out there that week to look for you, but he didn't find you."

The man didn't find me because he was looking for *Martin McCloud*, not *Mitchell Jordanger*. Mike had told Eric where I was but he didn't tell him I had changed my name. That was probably to protect Sonny because he had given me my alias. Over the years I had wondered who sent that guy. Now I knew that it was Eric and Mike all along.

Eric was looking a little shaky but he kept the shotgun pointed at my chest. I had to keep him talking to distract him from pulling the trigger.

"I'm sorry about Vince and Dave but these past years haven't been easy for me either, Eric. I never did anything musically to speak of after the Henley-McCloud Band. I own a poorly performing record store, and I have a job that I hate. There's never been anyone else for me since Mia died. The woman I'm with now doesn't even know the real me."

"Poor you," he slurred.

Now was the time to get the gun. I hadn't really relaxed in the armchair when I sat down. I had kept my feet planted hard on the floor so I could spring if I got the chance. Eric, drunk and visibly tired, relaxed for a second so I seized my opportunity. I lunged forward with everything I had. Eric jumped with surprise as I came across the desk. As the force of my body crashed over him, his chair fell backward and we both slammed to the floor. We pushed the shotgun up between us and fought each other hard to get control. I finally managed to wrestle it out of his hands and viciously slammed the butte into his cheek. He collapsed and moved no more.

I stood over his motionless body still breathing hard from the scuffle. If I didn't kill Eric he would go to the police when he woke up. I bent down and felt his carotid artery. He was still alive. I walked around him and stood so that my feet were even with the top of his head. I knelt down and placed the shotgun cross-wise under his chin. I pressed it down on his neck. Like all the others, he woke up when he felt his life slipping away. He grabbed at my hands, but there was nothing that he could do. Soon he was lying still again, and when I checked his pulse this time there was nothing.

Chapter 17
Atlanta, Georgia, December, 2007

I'd been jumpy ever since Melanie and I had returned to Atlanta from Mobile. I couldn't get Eric out of my mind. The story of his murder had not been picked up by CNN or any other national news organization, so I had no way of knowing how the investigation was proceeding. I was so paranoid that the police were going to arrest me that I wouldn't even search for the story on-line. I felt angry about my predicament and a little depressed. After eighteen years of carefully planned and executed murders, I was back in the same boat I was in when I killed Delphine and Bates.

Everything in Mobile had gone wrong. First, the fat cop at his "pretend" road-block had identified me in my rental car. When that happened, it obliterated my first line of defense against getting caught. I was no longer anonymous. I *stood out* because I had pissed the cop off so badly. Then my second line of defense was destroyed when I ran into Eric. Unlike Vodronika and all the others, he wasn't someone who was unrelated to me. Third, he wasn't invisible to everyone around him. He was drinking in a community bar where he was well known and liked. I had spent many sleepless nights worrying about whether Wintzie or the bartender noticed that I followed Eric when he left the bar. If they did, they might have seen me leave in the Pathfinder. That would make two sightings of that damned rental car. I was also worried about Connie. Eric might have told her who I was when I followed them to her apartment. My DNA was surely all over Eric's body because of the fight we had. If the police had my DNA and my name to go with it, all they would have to do is connect the dots.

I tried to keep my mind off of it as I sat inside my cubicle at *Wilson's* on a Friday afternoon. We had gotten a job to outfit a high school with surveillance cameras, so I was reviewing a schematic of the school. Using my computer, I dropped cameras into locations on the schematic. Then I checked to see that all of the shots the client wanted to see would be captured.

Around me, Christmas lights twinkled and silver garlands shimmered under the florescent office lights overhead. Christmas Eve was just one week away, but I was too jumpy to take another chance. I had convinced Melanie that I wanted to celebrate at home so we wouldn't have to fly out of town. She believed my story just like she always did, and then she went crazy with excitement. She had decorated every inch of our house and put up a huge Christmas tree. Then she went outside and strung lights on every tree and shrub. When I saw our yard, I was glad it was dormant because of the humiliation she had subjected it to. It looked like it belonged on the Vegas strip. In typical Melanie fashion, she had gone completely overboard and she was still finding new ways to obsess. Her latest preoccupation was with serving the perfect Christmas dinner.

Nikki, my companion Sales Engineer, sat in the cubicle next to mine. She was a loud woman ordinarily; more comfortable on a job-site than in an office so I wasn't surprised when I overheard her arguing with someone on her phone. The argument seemed to be about the condition of her yard. She was angrily quoting codes about things like the height of grass and whether or not lawn chairs were considered garbage. I figured that the person on the other end of the line was from the local county office. After a few more minutes of arguing, I heard Nikki slam down her phone. Then she noisily rolled her chair into my cubicle.

"Those SOB's aren't going to tell me what I can do in my own damn yard!" she yelled.

"You can't fight city hall, Nikki," I told her without looking away from my computer screen.

"You two want to grab a drink after work?" Lauren asked.

I turned around at the sound of her voice. She was standing in the doorway of my cubicle just behind Nikki.

"My daughter is visiting her grandma this weekend so I'm free," she explained.

I would have liked to go with Lauren to have a drink to soothe my nerves, but Melanie was at home making a "preliminary Christmas dinner". She had invited some friends of ours' from the neighborhood, and I knew I would never hear the end of it if I was late.

"I can't," I said. "Melanie is at home making a "practice" dinner so she'll be ready for Christmas Day. She's nervous about cooking for her family next week, so she's doing a trial run tonight."

"I'll go with you, Lauren," Nikki said.

"All right," Lauren told her. "I'll be ready to leave in twenty minutes. Let's go to *Diggers*, O.K?"

Nikki nodded at Lauren and then proceeded to roll her chair back into her own cubicle. Lauren stepped aside to let her pass.

"Did I hear you correctly?" Lauren asked. "Are you and Melanie spending Christmas at home this year?"

"Yep, we're trying something different this year," I said, trying to sound casual.

"Well, I think that's great. I hope you both have a wonderful holiday."

"Thanks," I replied. *I just hope I don't spend it in jail*, I thought.

I looked back at Lauren sharply to see if she had read my thoughts. She returned my gaze with a quizzical expression.

"Mitch, are you all right? You suddenly looked pale," she said.

"Uh, yeah, everything's fine," I replied.

"Are you sure? You really look like you're not feeling well-"

"I better get going," I said hastily. "Melanie will kill me if I'm late."

Lauren nodded and watched me while I shut my laptop down and then slid it inside my bag. I was starting to feel annoyed. I felt like I was under a microscope.

"Goodnight, Nikki," I called as I got up from my desk.

"Goodnight, Mitch," she replied. "And listen, tell Melanie not to worry so much. I'm sure her dinner will turn out just fine."

Lauren stood to one side of my cubicle doorway to let me pass.

"Have a good weekend," she said, "Tell Melanie I wish her the best of luck with her dinner."

"I will," I said.

As I rode the elevator down to the first floor, a terrifying feeling came over me. I was suddenly convinced that the police were waiting for me outside. My hand shook when I pushed the building's glass door open, and then relief flooded over me when I saw that they weren't there. I walked over to my truck, got inside quickly, and then gunned it accidentally as I backed out because I was so anxious to get out of there. On the way home I nearly wrecked because I made the trip with my eyes glued to the rear-view mirror. Finally, I made the familiar left turn into my subdivision.

When I came to a stop sign a few yards from my house, I glanced over at it as I hit my brakes. My heart began to pound again when I saw that my nightmare was really coming true. Two police cars were sitting in my driveway. It felt like a dream at first, but I soon recovered. I had prepared for this possibility like an athlete prepares for a race. I immediately threw my cell phone out of my window so the police couldn't track my movements by it, and then I made a right and drove in the opposite direction. I drove through my neighborhood along a road that circled behind my house. When I got to a spot that allowed me to see my backyard, I strained to see anything that would tell me what was going on inside. Everything looked like it always did. I saw the sloped roof of the shed where I kept my music equipment and a few branches of the Crape Myrtle tree where I had buried Ralphie. Instead of completing the circle that would take me back around to my house, I went straight and exited the subdivision from another entrance.

I drove away from home on frost covered roads as the sun relinquished its rights to the day. Fading orange light streaked across frozen yards. Even though it wasn't quite dark yet, most of the other drivers I passed had already turned on their headlights. They were probably headed home from work or Christmas shopping, but I was on the road for a much more sinister reason. I was driving to the *Night Owl* so I could get the cash I had stashed there.

When I pulled up in front of my store, I was glad for once that there weren't any customers. The place was totally dark. The kid who managed it must have closed up early for the night. I hurriedly went inside to my office where I kept the cash inside a portable safe. I opened the safe and pulled out the same duffel bag I had used when I fled to St. Thomas in the 1970s. It contained nearly $70,000.00. It what was what remained of the money that I had stolen from Eric, Vince, and Dave. I grabbed the bag of cash and got the hell out of there.

Back on the road, I wasn't sure where I should go. I had always planned to get the cash and drive straight out of town if the police came looking for me, but I felt like I needed to gather my thoughts first. After all, I wasn't a kid anymore and, truthfully, I didn't want to run again. I remembered Lauren had said that she and Nikki were going to *Diggers*. I would go there for a while. That would buy me some time because no one would think to look for me there.

Diggers was a small place that was tucked in between two shopping plazas. Fortunately for me, it wasn't visible from the main road. When I pulled into the parking lot, I spotted Lauren's Honda and Nikki's pick-up right away. I parked next to them, grabbed the duffel bag of cash, and then hastily walked inside. When I first walked in, I only saw the bartender polishing a glass behind the bar. Then I heard Nikki's loud laughter. I followed the sound until I saw her and Lauren sitting in a booth. Nikki's back was to me, but Lauren looked surprised when she saw me.

"Mitch! What are you doing here? I thought..."

"Melanie and I had a fight," I explained as I slid into the booth next to Nikki. I put the duffel bag down on the seat between us.

"Well, in that case, let's get another round," Nikki said gleefully. "Hey!" she exploded at the bartender across the room. "Get us another round and get my friend here whatever he wants!"

"Scotch," I said apologetically.

Nikki was a kind person deep down, but she sometimes had a way of putting people off. The bartender looked irritated and I was worried because I didn't want to stand out. I could just imagine him seeing my picture on the news later and then remembering me because of Nikki. I tried to look calm as I sat there and listened to her and Lauren talk, but inside my mind was racing. I wanted to know what was going on back at my house. Poor Melanie. She had been looking forward to spending Christmas at home. She had worked so hard, but now her dinner party and her holiday were ruined. I imagined her sitting alone in our dining room with all the food she had prepared spread out on the table before her. She was sobbing because there was no one to appreciate her efforts except for the police in the next room.

"Did she kick you out?" Nikki blurted.

"W-what?" I asked. I had been deep in my own thoughts.

"The bag," she said balefully as she jerked her thumb toward it. "Did Melanie make you pack a bag and get out?"

"Uh, something like that," I said as I nervously ran my hand over the zipper.

"You musta done something bad to make her kick you out so close to Christmas," Nikki continued.

"Nikki, leave Mitch alone!" Lauren interrupted. "He probably doesn't want to talk about it."

"Sorry," Nikki said. "You're welcome to stay at my house if you want." She drummed her fingers on the table and then leaned back. "Well, what do you guys think? Another round or what?"

"Not for me, Nikki," Lauren told her. "I've had three already."

While we waited for our tab, I was already busy thinking about where I would go next. I could take Nikki up on her offer to stay with her, but I wasn't sure that I could trust her. After the bartender brought our change, we left the tip and walked outside. It felt like the temperature had dropped at least ten degrees. The night air was cold and stinging.

"You two want to grab some dinner or something?" Nikki asked when we got to our cars.

I was about to say yes when she suddenly began to back-pedal.

"On second thought," she said, "I better call it a night. I've got to be up early tomorrow morning."

"Thanks for coming out tonight," Lauren told her.

Nikki nodded and got in her truck. I couldn't be sure, but I sensed that Lauren must have given her a look. I felt depressed as I watched Nikki drive away. I had no idea where I would go next.

"Mitch," Lauren said, "why don't you come to my place for a while? Corinne is still at her grandmother's, and I'm guessing that you don't want to go home just yet."

Relieved, I got in my truck and followed her.

Lauren's neighborhood consisted of tract houses that had been built in the 1950s. She told me once in a moment of frustration that it wasn't safe, but she had to rent there because of her financial problems. I knew she didn't like it but when I saw the house, I could tell that she had tried to make the most of it. It was a tiny, brick ranch that had been painted in a cream color and the shutters were painted black. It featured a dated picture window, a small cement porch with black metal railings, and a carport supported by black metal poles. Through the picture window I could just make out the dark shape of an unlit Christmas tree. The yard was dormant, but it looked like it was well-maintained. Azalea bushes that had quit blooming for the winter lined the front of the house, and a row of giant Frazier fir trees formed a natural fence between Lauren and her neighbor. I waited in my truck on the street while Lauren parked her car under her carport. I watched as she got out and hurriedly unlocked the side door to her house. She waved so I grabbed my duffel bag, resolutely got out into the cold, and sprinted over to her.

I followed her inside into a small living room that had a hardwood floor, ivory walls, and a built-in book case. Photos of Lauren's daughter, Corinne, sat on the shelves along with Christmas candles and several books that were carelessly arranged.

"Make yourself comfortable," Lauren said as she took off her coat.

She went over to the Christmas tree and plugged the electrical cord that dangled from it into an outlet. Tiny gold, blue, green, and red lights came on. The soft light was reflected on the picture window's glass.

Even in my panicky state, the soft lights from the tree and the small, cozy room were comforting. As I settled back onto Lauren's sofa, I felt more relaxed than I had in weeks.

"I turned up the heat," Lauren said as she briskly rubbed her hands together. "Can I take your coat?"

I peeled off my jacket and handed it to her. She disappeared with it and then I heard her hang it up inside a closet down the hall. When she reappeared she went over to a small mahogany side table. On top of it were four glass decanters that were each a different shape and style. Dark and light colored liquors shimmered inside each one.

"Mitch, I don't have any scotch," she said as she looked over the decanters, "but I've got whiskey, or I could make some coffee and put some Frangelico and Bailey's in it. Have you had that? It's wonderful."

"Sounds great," I said.

She nodded and disappeared into the kitchen. Soon the sounds of coffee chugging through an automatic coffee maker could be heard. The smell that permeated the living room was warm and intoxicating. After a few minutes, she reappeared with two over-sized mugs. She returned to her mahogany side table where she poured a shot from one of the decanters into each one.

"The Bailey's is already in there," she said. "I keep that in the refrigerator."

We sat before her tree sipping the wonderful concoction she had made. Now was the time to tell her everything. Deep down, I had known that I was going to confess if I found her that night. After she heard what I had to say, it would be her choice about whether to turn me in. Whatever she decided, though, I was not going to hurt her. She was my friend. She was the only person I had felt close to since Mia died.

I focused on Lauren's Christmas tree as I prepared to confess. As I stared at it, the words began to pour out of me like a fast moving river. I told her about the event that started everything; killing the pedophile at the pool when I was a kid. I explained how I couldn't lock up the darkness he had unleashed. I had fantasized about killing again until Mia and her family inspired me to be different. I lost them when I caused Mia to miscarry and eventually commit suicide. I told her how I killed Delphine and then faked my death by sinking the *Polargo* so I wouldn't be arrested. I even told her about the money I stole so I could get Sonny to help me and then escape to St. Thomas. It felt strange when I told her my real name was Martin Richard McCloud. I hadn't said that name out loud in twenty-nine years.

I told her how my friends in St. Thomas had turned on me after they found out I killed Bates. I spoke of the epiphany I had when I watched the old man row out into the harbor to become shark bait. It had reawakened my urge to kill. To keep from getting caught, I would choose inconsequential people who were just like the old man. I told her about the murders I committed every year at Thanksgiving and Christmas. Exhausted, I ended my confession by telling her about Eric's murder and that the police were probably looking for me.

At last I fell silent. I had spoken for hours, uninterrupted, in front of Lauren's softly lit tree. It seemed to have taken on the solemnity of a sacred altar. During my monologue, Lauren had listened quietly and periodically re-filled our mugs with coffee and liquor. I couldn't look at her while I confessed, but now I turned to face her at last.

Maybe she was drunk, but her face showed no fear. Her eyes were full of sympathy and kindness. To my surprise, she put her mug down and reached out to hug me. After a long embrace, she surprised me again with her question.

"Could you go back to St. Thomas now, do you think?"

I blinked hard. "What?" I asked.

"Could you go back to St. Thomas now? Would it be safe for you there? It's been twenty-eight years, after all."

I was shocked. Lauren was not the least bit interested in my moral failings; only in the practical side of what should be done now. I looked into her face again and saw that she was serious. Her attitude made me snap out of my remorseful mood, short-lived though it had been.

"I don't know," " I said, "I mean, it's not like it was back in the 70s. They didn't check things out back then like they do now after 9-11."

"If you did go back, could you hide out in one of those houses you told me about?" she asked.

There was a small chance that at least one of my houses was still standing and hadn't been taken over by squatters. If so, I could go back with the cash I had and live in one of them while I laid low. I wasn't worried about the guy who chased me out of there. He had been hired by Eric, so he was long gone and no longer a threat. There was always the possibility that I would run into one of my old friends like Sandro or Celine, but even if I did, they probably wouldn't recognize me. Lauren's idea was beginning to sound more and more appealing.

"You know, Lauren, I think I'd be willing to chance it."

"Me, too," she replied. "Corinne and I could go with you."

"What? You'd go with me? Why?"

"Mitch, what do I have here? A job that barely pays my bills, collection agencies calling me day and night, and a lunatic ex-husband who threatens me all the time. If we went with you, Corinne and I could get a fresh start. I would still have to find a job, but at least we would be living on a beautiful island far away from her crazy dad."

"What about joint custody?" I asked. "I thought you couldn't afford a lawyer to get full custody. Can you leave the state with Corinne?"

"Let me worry about that," Lauren said angrily. She pushed her shirt collar down to reveal a dark bruise. I had choked enough people to know what it meant. He had tried to strangle her.

"After what he did this time," she continued, "I'm not going to take his crap anymore. I took pictures. If he tries anything I'll take them to the police."

For the rest of the night we plotted about how we would go to St. Thomas to live. Lauren figured she and Corinne could join me in a month or two, but I needed to leave right away. She checked for flights on-line and found out that the next one left on Sunday. It was already 3 a.m. on Saturday morning, so we decided I would spend the rest of the weekend at her house. She would take me to the airport on Sunday morning and pick Corinne up on the way back. We thought it would be safe because no one would think to look for me there. However, neither of us was comfortable with my truck sitting on the street outside her house. We decided to drive it back to *Wilson's* and leave it in the parking lot.

Lauren unplugged the Christmas tree and went to get our coats. As we pulled them on, I told her to drive to an apartment complex behind *Wilson's* and wait for me there. I didn't want her car to be seen on any of *Wilson's* surveillance cameras. When I got to *Wilson's,* I parked in a spot that I knew the cameras couldn't see. I left my keys in the ignition, got out into the cold again, and jogged over to the fence behind the office. It backed up to the apartment complex where Lauren was waiting. I climbed over it and then carefully made my way down a small hill. I tried not to break my ankle on the sewer grating that I knew was lurking somewhere on the ground. I soon found Lauren and we drove back to her house, too wired and tense to sleep. We knew our plan was a house of cards. Of all the problems it had, however, Nikki was the most immediate. She had been with us at *Diggers*. If she told the police we were together it would be bad for Lauren. They would know she was with me on the night I disappeared.

When we got back to Lauren's house, she told me goodnight and went into her bedroom. I lay down on her sofa even though I didn't think I could sleep. However, I soon drifted off anyway and knew no more.

Chapter 18
Atlanta, Georgia, December, 2007

I awoke to the irritating feeling of someone tapping my shoulder hard. I jumped up in a panic thinking it was the police and then I almost went blind. Bright sunlight was pouring in through the picture window. When I gathered my wits, I realized that it was Lauren who had tapped on my shoulder. She had a very worried look on her face.

"A snow storm is coming," she said frantically. "The airport's website says every flight in or out is probably going to be cancelled! You could be stuck here for a week! Mitch, what are we going to do?"

Only a few hours had passed since we made our plans to go to St. Thomas, but already things were going wrong. Not only did I need to get out of town before the police stepped up their search, but Corinne would be coming home on Sunday.

"I know what to do," Lauren said more to herself than to me. "My grandmother owns a cabin up in the Blue Ridge Mountains. She usually rents it, but it should be vacant now. You can stay there until the storm clears. I'll get dressed and take you there."

The Darkness Behind the Door

    Soon we were in her car again, this time headed to her grandmother's cabin in the Blue Ridge Mountains of North Georgia. The further north we drove, the more rural and hilly it became. I stared out of the passenger-side window at the increasingly steep, blue mountains that peaked out through the morning fog. The sun was so bright and the sky was so clear that it was hard to believe a snow storm was on the way. Unfortunately, the blinding sunlight was doing nothing for my hang-over. I looked over at Lauren but she seemed to be lost in her own thoughts. She pushed in her car's cigarette lighter and then grimly lit her cigarette when it was ready. I felt the cold air creep in through her window when she cracked it to let the ashes fly out. I was about to tell her to pull over so we could get something to eat when a police cruiser pulled in behind us. Lauren gasped and I felt my empty stomach drop like a stone. The cop stayed behind us for six miles before he finally turned off, but those six miles had felt like six years. I didn't care about eating anymore and poor Lauren looked as white as a ghost. All I cared about now was getting to her grandmother's cabin so we would be safe.
    After what seemed like an eternity on the main highway, Lauren finally turned onto a tiny road that ran behind a small grocery store. She stayed on the tiny road for just a few minutes before she turned again onto Aska Road. We passed a sign that read "Chattahoochee National Forest." My nerves were frazzled but my spirits began to rise as we drove because of how beautiful and secluded it was. Except for the occasional cabin that peeked out from behind thick pine trees, it seemed like Lauren and I were the only two people in the world.
    The road began to narrow as we wound our way up through the mountains. Through my passenger-side window I saw beautiful green valleys and more trees. On Lauren's side of the road enormous gray boulders hung from overhead. Little streams of

water that ran alongside the road got stronger and stronger until they became a fast moving river. It rushed over smooth, black rocks that created glistening white-caps and dangerous looking rapids along the way. I could feel the intense cold coming off of it through Lauren's cracked window.

"That's the Toccoa River," Lauren said. "It runs behind the cabin, too, but it's not as strong there."

We drove on past a surreal-looking green pasture that was full of Black Angus cows and then crossed a small, covered bridge. Finally, Lauren slowed down so she could make a turn and drive down a steep gravel driveway. It led to a log cabin that was set several yards back from the road. The car rocked back and forth as she expertly guided it down the incline. At one point, her rear bumper scraped the ground but she didn't seem to mind. It was obvious she had done this many times before. Once she reached the bottom, she gunned the car and drove around back behind the cabin.

"This is it," she said as she turned off the engine. "Come on, we'll go out on the deck first so you can get a good look at the river."

I grabbed the duffel bag of cash and followed her as she walked past a screened-in porch to where a large deck stretched out over the river. I stood next to her near the railing and we both stared down at the cold, black water that rushed past our feet several feet below. Across the river, low hanging trees gracefully skimmed the water's surface. They seemed to be leaning over to give it a kiss.

"Beautiful, isn't it?" Lauren asked.

"Yes, very nice," I replied.

I looked at her strained face and wondered if she regretted helping me. After all, she had a child to think of.

"Thank you for bringing me here," I said.

She nodded and gave me a weary smile. "It's cold out here," she said. "Let's go inside."

We walked around to the front of the cabin. I watched her as she lifted a loose board from the porch. She took out a set of keys from underneath the board and then unlocked the front door. She walked inside ahead of me, flipping on lights as she went. She disappeared around a corner and then I heard and smelled a gas furnace come on. She had obviously turned on the heat. She reappeared and went into the kitchen where she opened the refrigerator door.

"Just as I thought," she said, "Nothing to eat. I'll have to go back into town later and get some supplies, but I've got to get some sleep first. Can you wait to eat or are you starving?"

I hadn't felt hungry since the cop drove behind us on the interstate.

"I'm fine," I said, "I could use some sleep, too."

"O.K, then," she replied, "I'll show you where the bedrooms are."

We left the kitchen with its outdated but clean appliances, and walked through a family room that had a stone fireplace, a plaid sofa, and a leather recliner. Large windows provided panoramic views of the river and the woods outside. Through them I could see the screened-in porch and the deck Lauren had shown me when we first arrived.

"The bedrooms and the bathroom are back here," Lauren said as she walked down a small hallway that led away from the family room. She opened the door to the first bedroom along the hall.

"Why don't you stay in this one?' she asked.

The room was furnished simply with a king-sized bed and a dresser that matched. Lauren walked over to a set of heavy curtains and pulled them back to reveal a sliding glass door. Through it I could see the porch and deck again.

"This room has access to the deck and the river through here," she said. "It will be cold, but you might want to go out there again after you wake up."

"Thanks," I said as I flopped down onto the bed.

Lauren walked over to the bed and sat down beside me.

"You know, Mitch, you might be stuck out here for a while if the weather gets as bad as they're predicting. I have to go home tomorrow to pick up Corinne and I don't know when I'll be able to come back. There is a phone here at the cabin, but we probably shouldn't talk on it in case the police are listening in."

The grim reality of my predicament washed over me like a rogue wave. When Lauren went home tomorrow, she was going to take the car. I would be stuck out here in the middle of nowhere with no way to escape. I realized I was going to be a sitting duck and it made me feel dangerously out of control. I should have felt grateful to Lauren but I was beginning to resent her instead.

"O.K.," I said casually to hide my real feelings.

Lauren nodded approvingly and patted my hand. "Well, I'm beat. I'll be down the hall if you need me."

She slipped out of the room. I heard her walk down the hall and open another door. Her situation was much more dangerous than she realized. She was alone with a killer who was starting to hate her. Suddenly, the room began to spin and I felt like I couldn't breathe. I gripped the mattress and stared at the floor in an effort to get my bearings. Sweat ran down my face so I ripped off my jacket and unbuttoned my shirt. A dark thought kept coming to me even though I tried to push it away. I wanted, ***needed***, to go into the bedroom where Lauren was sleeping and choke her to death. I would put my hands over the outline her ex-husband's hands had made and squeeze until she was dead. Then I could take her car and go anywhere I wanted. I should have stuck to my plan and left town after I got the cash from the *Night Owl*. I would be safe now if I had, but I was marooned in the woods instead.

Gradually, the room stopped spinning. I got up and walked over to the dresser so I could look in the mirror. My face looked pale and my eyes looked dark and dead. I forced myself to go outside so I wouldn't go into Lauren's bedroom and kill her. Back on the deck, the coolness coming off the Toccoa River calmed me. I willed the cold to numb my brain like a powerful neurotoxin. I stared down at the river until it hypnotized me. I focused on the sound of the rapids until everything else receded. I kept staring at the water until, to my horror, a woman floated up from the depths. She stared at me with unseeing eyes. It was Lauren. *Am I losing my mind?* I thought desperately. *Could I have killed Lauren already and blocked it out?*

I bolted back inside the cabin and walked down the hall to the bedroom I thought she was in. I pushed the door open slowly because I was afraid of what I would find. If she wasn't there, then her body really was floating in the river outside. After my eyes adjusted to the dim light in the room, I saw her small form lying on the bed. I listened until I heard her breathing and then I closed the door. Relieved but still shaken, I went into the family room and planted myself on the sofa. Two hours passed before Lauren woke up. She came into the family room looking somewhat rested but her expression was still strained. I must have looked bad, because when she saw me her strain became a full-blown panic.

"Did something happen?" she asked frantically. Her eyes shot over to the window. She looked at it as though she expected to see blue lights reflected off the blinds.

"Nothing happened," I lied.

Nothing had happened except that I had conjured the image of her dead body floating in the Toccoa River.

"Well, what is it then?" she asked as her eyes searched my face. "Did you get any sleep? You look awful."

"No, I didn't sleep," I said. I turned away from her because I couldn't look her in the eye. "I guess I'm too keyed up."

"You must be starving," she said sympathetically. "I'll go into town and get some food and supplies. Do you want anything in particular?"

"Scotch," I replied, "A big bottle."

"O.K., but it will take a while. This is a dry county so I'll have to drive back toward Atlanta to find a liquor store."

My heart started to pound again as she slipped her coat on and grabbed her keys. *What if she didn't come back?* When I watched her open the door, I willed myself to let her go. She seemed to sense my ambivalence because she looked back at me and gave me a reassuring smile.

"Don't, worry, Mitch. I **will** be back. You can count on it."

She closed the door to the cabin behind her. I wanted to believe her, but I felt like my coffin had just been hammered shut. When I heard her crank her car, my head felt like it was splitting in two. I lay back on the sofa in unbelievable pain with my thoughts and my pulse racing. I finally found relief by passing out.

When I opened my eyes again, the interior of the cabin was pitch black and it was dark outside.

"Lauren?" I called out into the black, empty room. There was no answer.

My headache had subsided down to a dull ache but the panicky, sick feeling was back. Lauren said she would have to drive for a while to find a liquor store, but it seemed like she had been gone too long. She must have turned me in after she realized what it was like to live on the run. Any minute now, the police were going to burst onto the property with their blue lights flashing, sirens blaring, and guns drawn. When I peered out of the window through the blinds, I saw a car turn into the driveway. When it got closer, I saw that it was Lauren's Honda and not the police. I listened as she parked her car but I still could not calm down. I waited for her just inside the door, wild-eyed and ready for a fight.

"Mitch!" she exclaimed when she saw me. "You scared me standing behind the door like that!"

We stood there staring at one another until she seemed to understand that she was in danger. I took an aggressive step toward her and she recoiled in fear. The look in her eyes reminded of how Celine had looked on the day she came to see me at *Jimmy's*. Somehow, though, Lauren seemed to change before my eyes. She suddenly looked strong and unafraid.

"Go and get the bags out of the car," she said evenly.

I took another step toward her, but she didn't flinch this time. I hesitated and then I walked around her and went outside. The air was cold and fresh. The grocery bags were sitting in the backseat of her car, but I passed them by and went out on the deck instead. I looked down at the cold water again, but this time Lauren's dead body did not appear. I breathed a sigh of relief and looked up at the night sky. The stars were the brightest that I had ever seen. Maybe the crisis had passed. Whatever happened now, I was determined to make sure that things worked out for me, Lauren, and Corinne. I wasn't going to go to prison and I wasn't going to end up in St. Thomas alone. I would get another chance. I would make damn sure of it.

It was nearly six months before Lauren and Corinne were able to join me in St. Thomas. Lauren and I didn't communicate during that time, but shortly after they arrived on the island she told me what happened back home. The police had gone to *Wilson's* to look for me, but they had only talked to the owner and not the employees. Lauren told me that Nikki, maybe because she was always ready to fight city hall, had told them nothing. They hadn't gone to her to ask questions, so Nikki hadn't gone to them to tell them what she knew.

Lauren had shown her ex-husband the photos of her bruises. She told him he wouldn't have to worry about it or pay child support anymore if he let them go. She said he made a few threats at first, but after he thought about it he decided to cooperate. She said the timing was lucky because he had found someone else. After all of the torture they had endured at his hands, it seemed he was no longer interested in them.

Melanie was predictably devastated, Lauren said, and she still didn't understand what happened. The police had not told her very much, but what they did tell her she steadfastly refused to believe. She stubbornly clung to the belief that it was all a big mistake. I was surprised to hear that she found solace by dating one of our neighbors. He had been invited to her dinner party on the night I disappeared. I wondered briefly if I wasn't the only one in our relationship who had kept secrets, but I sincerely wished her the best.

After I got to St. Thomas, I went to look at what remained of my businesses and properties. The building where my real estate brokerage was housed had been turned into a restaurant. The hut where my tourism and bar businesses used to be was gone, but the shed behind it was still standing. The St. Thomas government had put a padlock on it along with a *no trespassing* sign, but I planned to break into it one night anyway. After all, I could always use a good kayak.

The run-down little bungalow I used to live in had been taken over by squatters and the neighborhood had become dangerously violent. I was shocked to see the change. The area was poor back when I lived there, but my neighbors were good people. It wasn't worth the risk to try to live there because of Lauren and Corinne, and I didn't want to call attention to myself by evicting the squatters. I crossed it off my list and moved on.

The roof of the next property I looked at had fallen in and there was graffiti all over the walls. Only iguanas and rats lived in what was left. I crossed it off the list, too, and went to check out the only other house I owned. It was located high up in the hills. I had to drive along a steep mountain road that was poorly maintained to get to it, but when I found the house I saw that it had a roof and it was vacant. I worked on it night and day over the next six months to get it ready for Lauren and Corinne.

On the day Lauren called to let me know they were coming, I went to meet them at the St. Thomas airport feeling young again. I was about to start my new life. Things were going to work out, I could feel it. I was getting another chance after all. Everything was opening up for me again.

Acknowledgements

First and foremost, I would like to thank my dear husband, Enayat, for his love, support, and advice all through the writing of this book. I would like to thank my daughter, Anna, for her love and encouragement as well. I would like to thank my mother, Dianne Lapides, for her constant optimism and enthusiasm for the book even when I struggled to stay the course. Other people to thank are my father, John Edgar, for his constructive criticism as well as Richard Wright, Neva French, Carlton Powell, Don Bolden, Carol Mayer, Sandy Gurowski, Amelia Fusaro, Bret Rachlin, Malou Statt, and Hillary Rowe. I would like to thank Erich Colbert for his technical assistance and Jacqui Hesse for providing me with my first audience, which was an experience that has proved invaluable. I want to thank the following people for their love and support during a tough time when most of this story was written: Gertrude Day, Pauline Edgar, Bessiemere Oliver, Christa Norris, Stephen Norris, Deborah Norris, Henry Norris, Paula Edgar, Kathy Buckley, Essie Pigrom, Joan Gordon, and Alan Lapides. Finally, I would like to thank my editor, Laura Brown, as well as Stella Jackson and all the staff at American

Book Publishing for their invaluable guidance throughout the entire process of publishing this book.

Biography

Karen Oliver worked in the mortgage and banking industry for two decades before retiring as Vice President to have her second child and pursue her lifetime love of writing. She was born in the south and has lived in every southern city that the story, *The Darkness Behind the Door*, takes place in. She has served as a docent in historical homes and volunteers her time at various non-profit organizations. She resides in Marietta, GA with her husband and two daughters. This is her first novel.

Feedback Request

Thank you for purchasing my book. I hope you have enjoyed reading it as much as I enjoyed writing it.

Please take a moment and visit Amazon.com and insert the ISBN# 978-1-49368-215-7 in the search box. Feel free to express your thoughts and feelings both positive and negative. I deeply appreciate your feedback. While you are there, you may notice what others thought of my book as well. Perhaps your insights are shared with others.

Thank you in advance for taking the time to respond. I will check Amazon.com soon to read your response.

Made in the USA
Lexington, KY
03 April 2014